John Creasey – Master Storyteller

Born in Surrey, England in 1908 ii
there were nine children, John Crease͜ ͜ ͜ ͜ ͜p ͜o ͜e a true master story teller and international sensation. His more than 600
crime, mystery and thriller titles have now sold 80 million copies in 25 languages. These include many popular series such as
Gideon of Scotland Yard, The Toff, Dr Palfrey and *The Baron*.

Creasy wrote under many pseudonyms, explaining that booksellers
had complained he totally dominated the 'C' section in stores. They
included:

> *Gordon Ashe, M E Cooke, Norman Deane, Robert Caine
> Frazer, Patrick Gill, Michael Halliday, Charles Hogarth,
> Brian Hope, Colin Hughes, Kyle Hunt, Abel Mann, Peter
> Manton, J J Marric, Richard Martin, Rodney Mattheson,
> Anthony Morton* and *Jeremy York*.

Never one to sit still, Creasey had a strong social conscience,
and stood for Parliament several times, along with founding the
One Party Alliance which promoted the idea of government by
a coalition of the best minds from across the political spectrum.

He also founded the British Crime Writers' Association, which to this
day celebrates outstanding crime writing. The Mystery Writers of
America bestowed upon him the Edgar Award for best novel and then
in 1969 the ultimate Grand Master Award. John Creasey's stories are as
compelling today as ever.

THE TOFF SERIES

The Toff

and

The Terrified Taxman

John Creasey

This edition published in 2012 by House of Stratus, an imprint of Stratus Books Ltd., Lisandra House, Fore Street, Looe, Cornwall, PL13 1AD, U.K.
www.houseofstratus.com

Typeset by House of Stratus.

A catalogue record for this book is available from the British Library and the Library of Congress.

ISBN 07551-2398-0
EAN 978-07551-2398-8

In life, it is said, it is the taxman who has become virtually an instrument of terror by extortion – a most unjust indictment of Inspectors and Collectors who are simply doing their job. I hope those who read this book will hereafter bend a more kindly eye upon all taxmen, to whom it is dedicated with apologies for any errors I may have made in depicting the way they handle our returns.

John Creasey

CHAPTER I

The Taxman

It was the Toff's first visit to this particular taxman.

On the wall-plate by the open front door of the Victorian building in Mayfair where the taxman had his offices, he was much more comprehensively described, of course. This modest plaque read:

Inland Revenue
H.M. Inspector of Taxes
4th Floor

Above, below and on either side of this announcement were other plaques. Two banks had offices here; so did three firms of accountants, two insurance brokers, one insurance company, a number of business firms trading from such goods as engineering small parts, imported fruit, machine-tool makers to toy manufacturers. And, tucked away on the seventh and top floor, were:

Johnny P. Rains
Private Investigator
and
Bonatti and Firmani
Artists in Decor

Not unnaturally, the Toff was more interested in Johnny P. Rains, the private investigator who made himself so familiar with clients even before they became clients.

"Johnny," a suspicious husband might say, "I want evidence to prove that my wife is unfaithful to me," and there seemed no reason at all why Johnny P. Rains should refuse to help. However, the Johnnies of today's England were running into squalls. The law had decreed that inability to live together after trying over a reasonable period should be the favourite ground for divorce, with adultery an also ran; so where would the private eyes be now, poor things?

The Toff was inside the tall, dark entrance hall waiting for the large lift to descend carrying passengers behind the criss-cross iron bars of the car. A carload would surely soon arrive. He was never quite sure that a human being would in fact emerge when those doors opened; he half-expected an orang-utan, a baboon or, in those moments of the highest flights of fancy, a man from Mars. He was not exactly fanciful this fine April morning, however: more reflective and wary, for he had come to see his taxman and try to get what seemed to him a much fairer assessment of tax than the Inspector himself thought just.

Normally his, the Toff's, accountant would have been here, while the taxpayer disported himself or did good deeds, or even led his usual, everyday life, which was at times much less romantic than most people who knew him believed. Now and again recollection of the pounds and new pence involved came to him, only to be sternly if subconsciously suppressed by thoughts of other things and other people.

Johnny P. Rains, for instance.

He had heard, vaguely, of this Johnny.

Johnny P. had once worked for a client whose then wife had, in a manner of speaking, been represented by the Toff; she had been in fear of murderous assault from her husband, and couldn't he, Mr. Rollison, help her? *Please.* The details of the case were vague but doubtless would grow clearer if he dwelt on them. At the moment, however, he was coming to the stage when he would really have to think about his income tax figures.

"Rolly," his accountant-cum-friend of long standing had begged hoarsely from his sickbed, "don't start a slanging match, or tell the Inspector what you think of the Government. Just use sweet reason, if you must go and see him before I've recovered from this blasted back."

The accountant had a slipped disc.

"I always use sweet reason," the Toff had replied with great dignity.

"Perhaps you do," the accountant conceded, "but there's nothing like an Inspector of Taxes who sits like Buddha behind his desk and quotes the latest Finance Act at one, to make a layman lose his temper."

"I shall not lose my temper," the Toff had asserted.

I must not lose my temper, he thought, as he took a firmer grip on a slender briefcase which slid down from beneath his arm. Then in a flash of exasperation he muttered: "Where the devil is that lift?"

A man whom he had not heard approach, spoke from one side.

That in itself was enough to startle the Toff, who had heard no one approach. But here was the man, on his left and a few inches further back. As the Toff turned his head, the man said: "It is probably held up by a taxpayer who has fainted after his interview." There was a glimmer of humour in his blue-grey eyes. The man had a pleasant face, with broad features and a broad chin with an unexpected point. "You wouldn't prove to be of such a frail nature, would you, Mr. Rollison?"

Rollison, a tall, lean, dark-haired, very handsome man with an air of the gallant about him, pursed his lips and replied; almost sure that he was right about the identity of this man.

"I am about to find out, Mr. Rains."

"I'm disappointed," returned Johnny P. Rains. "I'd hoped you were coming to see me. Will you think me impertinent if I offer you a little advice?"

"Certainly not, but I can probably anticipate it," replied the Toff, whose real name was the Honourable Richard Rollison, "I must not lose my cool."

"Right!" confirmed Johnny P. Rains. "And at the same time, wrong. I can tell you in confidence that one Income Tax Inspector, no longer with us, told me, when we were together in the loo, that he always regarded loss of temper as an indication of guilt or concealment, and as a result, probed more deeply than he normally would. The new man hasn't said this so bluntly, but I suspect it's a general rule. Probably paragraph 7, sub-section 18, page 12 of the Income Tax Inspector's secret manual."

"Oh," said Rollison, raising his eyebrows in surprise. "Is there such a thing?"

"I've never seen one," answered Johnny P. Rains, "but I would be surprised if one doesn't exist."

"I shall look out for it," promised Rollison.

"Do tell me if you set eyes on it," pleaded the other. "Ah! I hear the lift. Probably some chit of a girl child has been holding the gates open for her boss, who is doubtless dictating at furious speed to his secretary."

"Or on the telephone," replied Rollison.

At that moment, the lift appeared in view, just above their heads. Inside were two pairs of legs – one pair trousered, one pair pantyhosed. This pair was on tiptoe. It was a remarkable, not to say a beautiful, sight. The remarkable fact was the way those legs seemed to stretch, from small feet and nice ankles up slender calves and even nice knees, to broadening thighs. The lift descended so slowly that the expanse of leg seemed to lengthen and lengthen. However, the girl wasn't all legs. She had a slim body pressed against a slender young man. They were in a close, kissing embrace and apparently oblivious of the two men at the gates.

The lift stopped. Johnny P. Rains opened the doors. The couple gave each other another hug and then, arms intertwining in such a way that it seemed as if their bodies were too, they came out, the girl looking up and the boy looking down. It was doubtful whether they noticed either Rollison or Rains, who stood obligingly on one side.

"My!" exclaimed Johnny.

"Sweet young love," murmured Rollison, stepping into the lift.

"They've probably realised they'll get a tax saving if they marry early rather than late," said Johnny, closing the doors. "Did you know that after a certain income level, it used to pay a couple to live in sin?"

4

"Fascinating," remarked Rollison as the lift crawled upwards. At a landing stood an infuriated man who cried: "Can't you stop that bloody thing here for once?" In a reflex action Johnny P. Rains pressed the 'stop' button and the lift stopped only an inch or two above the landing level; and the gates opened, the inside one at Johnny's thrust, the outside one at the older man's pull.

He came in, limping, not only old but grey.

"Thank you, thank you! Getting this infernal contraption to stop at the second floor is the nearest thing I know to the impossible. Thank you, thank you."

Both Johnny P. Rains and the Honourable Richard Rollison murmured the appropriate remarks and eventually the lift stopped at the fourth floor. Rollison stepped out. The private investigator continued upwards with the old man, who still looked exasperated. It was probably a chronic cast of countenance by now. Rollison saw the same wording on a smaller plaque on a door on the right of the lift, and went towards it. Inside was a cramped waiting room which looked rather like a doctor's or a dentist's, and a panel of glass in a green painted wall which held the single word:

ENQUIRIES

On one side was a bell push. Rollison pushed. There was no immediate response. Rollison waited long enough to see some notices stuck on the wall behind him, and was about to ring again when the glass panel slid open. At the same moment the door behind him opened and someone else stepped in.

"Good morning," a girl at the panel said. "Can I help you?"

She was young and pretty and pleasant and she had long golden hair.

"I've an appointment with Mr. Watson," said Rollison.

"Oh," breathed the girl. "You're the *Toff.*" She uttered the word with a kind of sibilance which was obviously meant to be heard by other girls sitting at desks behind her, and four heads turned: a dark one, a fair one, a red one and a grey. Rollison learned again what it meant to be the cynosure of all eyes.

He gave his nicest smile.

"How very nice to be recognised," he said.

"Oh, *everyone* was thrilled when they knew you were coming," the receptionist declared. She wore a knitted yellow sweater which fitted bosom-snug. "I'll tell Mr. Watson," she promised. "He won't keep you a minute, I'm sure."

She disappeared, leaving the panel open, while the four women stared at Rollison, and one began to rise from her chair. He noticed her pick up a pen as the man who had come in spoke from behind Rollison in the now familiar voice of Johnny P. Rains.

"Mr. R.," he said, "I wonder if you could spare me a few minutes after you've finished here. I'm only three floors up, and with any luck the lift will work."

Rollison, having no other engagements until after lunch, replied formally that he would be glad to. The woman who had picked up a pen was now at the open window, a plump and nicely made-up woman in her thirties.

"Mr. R., *could* I have your autograph, please?"

He signed a sheet of buff-coloured paper, then three more sheets as they each staked a claim; at last the blonde girl returned to announce that Mr. Watson would be glad to see him. But there was a change in her which Rollison was quick to notice. Something or someone had upset her, and who could it be but Mr. Watson? She had a rather scared look, which made her face more striking than attractive. Was he wrong? he wondered as she turned to lead the way. She wore a dress which fell below her knees, and was no doubt wise, for she had rather thick legs with over-full calves and her knees were probably enormous.

She led the way through a long, narrow office, where perhaps twenty girls and six men sat at small desks or typing tables, with piles of thick files about them. The whole length of one wall was shelved from floor to ceiling, and each shelf was piled high with these files, doubtless the dossiers, as it were, of taxpayers whose taxes were weighed and measured here.

Every head turned to look at the Toff, but the Toff behaved most circumspectly, following close on the fair girl's heels. She reached a door marked: *H. M. Inspector — Private*, tapped and stood aside.

A man called: "Come in," and she opened the door and the Toff went in.

Immediately, he realised that something was badly wrong. For this man had a frightened expression, reminding him vividly of the girl's: it was as if the same thing had scared them both. It was obvious, however, that Mr. Frederick Watson was doing his best to conceal his feelings. He stood up and proffered a hand and said with commendable heartiness: "Good morning, Mr. Rollison. May I say what a great pleasure it is to meet you?"

"May I say how much I hope that pleasure is going to be mutual?" replied Rollison, as they shook hands.

The remark appeared to puzzle the Inspector.

"I see, I see," he said; and then he gave a broader, more natural smile, and repeated with much greater vehemence born of real understanding. "I *see*! Well, you can be sure of this - do sit down - no one in this office wants you to pay a penny more than is lawfully due. That goes for everyone, including ourselves. *We* pay taxes, too, you know."

He tried to laugh: but failed. He pushed his chair back, brushing one hand across his forehead as he did so, and turned his swivel chair, which squeaked. Piled high on shelves behind him were dossiers like those in the other room, and Rollison assumed that these were the files of taxpayers whose obligations were now under review. On the man's desk was a fat file with a name written clearly in black. Even upside down, it was easy to read:

Rollison, Richard, the Hon.

But Watson looked on shelf after shelf, keeping his face averted, until suddenly he took out a big white handkerchief, and blew his nose with a loud honking. Almost at once he turned round, dusting his nose, then started back as if in astonishment.

"Here's your file, Mr. Rollison!"

"Is it really?" murmured Rollison.

"It is indeed," Watson blew again but with much less conviction.

"Hay fever, always get it in the Spring, not a cold, I assure you, only hay fever. Not at all contagious!" He pulled his chair closer to the desk. "I am sorry to hear about Mr. Slazenger, I do hope he recovers quickly. Has he tried an osteopath, I wonder? Some osteopaths are very good, I believe, on slipped discs and bad backs. Now, ah—*your* file, Mr. Rollison. Yes. I have a letter from Mr. Slazenger saying you would come to discuss your tax, and of course I am open to discussion: eager for it, in fact. The letter—" He placed his billowing handkerchief over his mouth and nose, so that only his eyes were free, and stared down at the letter on top of the pile of letters and forms in the case. "The letter says that you feel you have not been allowed sufficient expenses, on the one hand, and that you have been taxed on all your income as if it were unearned, whereas in fact you claim that a certain proportion *is* earned, and so taxable at a lower rate. If you care to tell me how much *you* feel is justifiable as a claim for expenses, business expenses, then perhaps we can reach a figure satisfactory to us both. I—"

The telephone bell rang, at his desk.

It startled the Toff, but it startled the Inspector much more. He went pale, and for a moment stared at the instrument without moving. At last, he stretched out for it, but there was no doubt in Rollison's mind that he was afraid of what it might be. He was a spare-boned man with a rather shiny jaw and nose, and his cheeks were slightly sunken.

"This is the Inspector," he announced.

Then he closed his eyes. And listened. His left hand was clenched on the desk, the knuckles looking white and huge. He moistened his lips as he muttered: "Very well. Very well. I'll look into it."

Slowly, he replaced the receiver. His hand was trembling, and his lips, too, as if he were under such strain that he could not keep still. He looked everywhere but at Rollison and then suddenly and over-boldly at him, and he gasped in a cracked voice: "Why on earth did you have to come here? Why on earth did you have to come?"

Chapter 2

The Terror

The truth was that Rollison had come because he was curious about the ways of income tax inspectors, and all knowledge was interesting and most of it useful. He could have left the matter with Slazenger, the expert, but he himself planned an early visit to the United States, and would like to get the matter settled before he left. For the amount of tax involved being some ten thousand pounds, was a large sum even for a man who was well endowed with this world's goods.

He did not answer that cry of despair, but sat back, feeling embarrassed and yet looking straight into Watson's eyes. They were rather small and deep-set, and a periwinkle blue, most vivid but shadowed because of dark patches beneath them, and ridges of skin and countless crows' feet. Those eyes, in fact, seemed much older than the rest of Mr. Watson, and they reflected deep, deep trouble.

Watson moistened his lips, shifted in his chair, looked right and left and then back at the Toff.

"I—I—I'm sorry," he muttered. "I shouldn't have said that."

"Perhaps it's a good thing that you did," replied Rollison. "I may be able to help."

"No!" cried Watson. "That's the last thing—" He broke off, gulped, and went on miserably: "I don't mean to be rude, Mr. Rollison, but I am—er—suffering from a great shock. An emotional disturbance, I—" He stopped, obviously not knowing how to go on, and then he simply sat back in his swivel armchair with its padded leather arms, and looked miserably at Rollison. His posture, chest curved inwards, made Rollison understand how thin he was; and now that Rollison began to take notice of the man other than his face and his manner, he saw the way the skin bagged under his chin as well as his eyes; how large his jacket was for him, how loose his collar with the neatly knotted grey tie; he had lost weight suddenly, probably recently.

The telephone bell rang again, and Watson started up and looked towards it; there was no doubt at all that he was terrified. He did not even move his hand, and soon the bell rang again.

"Er—excuse me," muttered Watson, gulping again. He stretched out with trembling hand, picked up the receiver, and croaked: "Hallo."

He listened intently, gradually relaxing; he sank back into the chair, telephone cable stretched as far as it would go.

"Yes," he said. "Yes ... Is Mr. Cobb free? ... Yes, I agree." There was a fervent note in his voice. "Yes, do." He rang off, wiped his forehead with the back of his hand, then sat up with a curious expression on his face; almost sly. He placed his large and bony hands on the Toff's file, and spoke in a stronger voice than he had yet used with the Toff. "I am extremely sorry, Mr. Rollison, but an urgent matter has occurred—er, cropped up—at my Head Office in Whitehall, and I have to go and discuss it with my superiors. My second-in-command here, Mr. Cobb, will be glad to help you in any way he can. I couldn't be more sorry but I'm sure you will understand."

What the Toff understood was that Mr. Watson was both relieved and delighted at this chance to get away from him. Instead of saying so, he got up as Watson rose to his feet, saying: "Of course, Mr. Watson. But I'll gladly come back at a more convenient time for you."

"No!" Alarm sprang back to Watson's eyes. "No," he went on more calmly, "I'm sure Mr. Cobb will be able to settle all the outstanding problems with you. I'll have a word with him before I go."

Watson rounded the desk and shook hands, leaving Rollison with an impression of a firm but cold and damp hand, then went out as if he couldn't escape quickly enough. The door closed with a decided snap, leaving Rollison entombed, as it were, in a cellar of other peoples' tax affairs. Watson was almost certainly breaking the rules. Rollison stood undecided for perhaps thirty seconds, staring at another door on the left of Watson's desk. If he had the true picture of the layout of these offices, that door led into a passage which in turn led to the landing where the lift was. There was a key in the lock.

On the thirty-first second, Rollison moved.

He reached the door, turned the key, opened the door and stepped out into a green painted, stone-floored passage. He closed the door softly and then hurried on tiptoe towards the landing, and ignoring the lift gates, raced up the stairs. At the top landing, he was only slightly breathless.

A door on the right was marked *Bonatti and Firmani, Artists in Decor,* and on the left was the name *Johnny P. Rains.* Rollison opened the door and found a small office, empty except for a desk, a chair, a telephone and a filing cabinet. Ahead was another door, marked *Private.* Rollison strode towards it, calling: "Mr. Rains!"

If Johnny P. was having a little peccadillo with his secretary, at least there was time for them to get out of a clinch before he pushed open the door.

Johnny P. Rains was alone, rising from a very large desk in a very small room which was lined impressively with books, mostly leather-bound. In contrast to the bleak little office outside there was an air of opulence here, especially noticeable in two brown leather armchairs and the desk furniture, all leather-topped.

"My goodness!" exclaimed Johnny P. "That was quick. Don't say he *did* throw you out!"

"Can you take a job at once?" demanded Rollison.

"This very second," flashed Johnny P. Rains.

"Watson is leaving the building. I'd like to know where he goes, whom he meets, what time he gets back. Will you get in touch with me at my flat?" As he spoke he turned on his heel and hurried out, down the stairs, along the passage. He opened the side door to Watson's office, closed it, but did not have time to turn the key before a footstep sounded at the outer office door. He did not even have time to sit down, only to reach his chair, before the other door opened.

If the man who appeared was surprised to see him standing, he showed no sign.

"Good morning, Mr. Rollison. I'm sorry to keep you waiting."

"You haven't been long," Rollison murmured.

"Do sit down." The man who was to deputise for Watson motioned to the chair by Rollison, and rounded the desk to Watson's place. He was a nondescript man, a smallish man, with thinning, greying hair and lined, weather-worn features: and obviously an outdoor man, Rollison was sure, probably one who sailed in small boats every moment he could spare. His eyes, wide-set, were the brown of newly husked chestnuts. He had a droll-looking mouth with deep lines, slightly like a withered bloodhound.

"Mr. Watson had been looking forward to meeting you for so long," he said. "But when a summons comes from on high, there is no arguing."

"Needs must when the devil drives," Rollison said, with an almost ludicrously straight face.

"Exactly," said Mr. Cobb, obviously glad to settle for any cliché. "I think I will be able to discuss your tax affairs with you intelligently, though. I worked a great deal on them before our change of Inspector."

"Oh, indeed. So you're familiar with my affairs."

"Possibly even more familiar than Mr. Watson." The brown eyes glinted.

"Happy day," murmured Rollison, relaxing in his chair.

"What exactly *is* your query?" Cobb asked, opening the file and sitting squarely in front of the desk.

"I have been over-taxed," declared Rollison, solemnly.

"A great number of taxpayers have been," stated Cobb, serenely.

"Surely that's a bit hard?" said Rollison.

"Oh, it always comes out in the wash, sir!"

"Not too late, I trust," Rollison said. "I'd rather discover any errors in my assessment before I pay any money."

"Very wise," approved Cobb, "*Very* wise indeed."

There was a quietly hearty manner in the man; as if he felt inwardly exuberant but knew that he had to prevent it from showing. Why, wondered Rollison, should he feel exuberant? For personal reasons? For professional? Speculation might be a waste of time, but this was a puzzle, on a lower key, like the one over Mr. Watson. Just as Watson had appeared almost pathetic, even pitiable, this man was likeable. His mouth was not only large but very mobile; bloodhound-shaped much of the time.

"Thank you," murmured Rollison.

"What exactly do you think we've done wrong?" asked Cobb.

"Over-assessed me," Rollison answered.

"By how much?"

"About a hundred per cent."

"Double what you expected it to be," remarked Cobb.

"That's rather a lot. And even what you expect is plenty, isn't it."

"It's ten thousand pounds," observed Rollison.

"And we've assessed you at twenty thousand?"

"Yes."

"Sure your sins haven't found you out?" demanded the Deputy Inspector.

For the first time, Rollison felt a reaction. They had been fencing, and he thought he knew why: Cobb was proving that he was as good as the next man, was showing that whatever the rest of the staff felt, he wasn't over-impressed by the Toff. But this was going too far. "Sure your sins haven't found you out?" was in fact offensive, no matter how facetiously it may have been intended. For the first time it occurred to Rollison that there might be much more in this assessment than a simple error. He recalled Slazenger's urgent exhortation not to lose his temper, but that didn't mean that he had to act as if he were either a dimwit, or was deliberately anxious not to offend.

"Sins," he echoed, carefully.

"Just a figure of speech, sir!" Cobb was quick with that assurance.

"Surely a very odd figure," Rollison retorted coldly. "Exactly what did you mean, Mr. Cobb?"

"Really, I wasn't serious."

"What a pity," Rollison said, and unexpectedly gave his brightest smile. "I am. What kind of 'sins' are committed by your taxpayers, Mr. Cobb?"

"Well, er! there *are* attempts at tax evasion you know."

"I have heard of them. Are you implying that I am making such an attempt?"

There was a long silence. At last, Cobb appeared to be completely serious as if he saw nothing remotely funny in the situation which Rollison had forced. Now that his full lips were set and straight, they didn't seem so large. He looked not so much droll as pug-like. There was no good-humoured gleam in his eyes. There *was* a kind of defiance, and in fact pugnacity about his whole face.

At last, he answered: "No, Mr. Rollison. But there is a great deal of ignorance of the tax laws, and mistakes are very easy to make."

"Not by certified accountants like Mr. Slazenger," Rollison countered.

"No. No, of course not! I—ah—I used a word injudiciously, Mr. Rollison, and I am sorry." Cobb opened the file, now very business-like. "There was not the slightest intention on my part to impugn your integrity, but even with the best of accountants, mistakes can be made." He pursed his lips upwards, then let them droop. *"Hmm."* He rolled his lips as if they were made of rubber. *"Hmm."* He set his lips and turned pages, as if he were anxious to put and to keep Rollison on edge. *"Hmm"* he repeated, and at last looked up. "It does appear that you have been under-assessed for several years, Mr. Rollison, and that certain allowances which had been made were not indeed allowable items, while some income claimed as earned has in fact not been. These present figures show a revised assessment to cover under-assessment for four years."

Rollison thought: This can't be true.

But Cobb was undoubtedly serious and would hardly make up a situation: it must appear to be in front of him. There was sternness in his expression, now, all the good humour and exuberance gone. Rollison felt, suddenly, as if he were on trial. It was absurd, of course, he hadn't declared false figures, but – *he* hadn't made out his own income tax returns, either; he had given the information to

Slazenger, and simply signed the form.

Could Slazenger—

Nonsense! he told himself. Slazenger couldn't possibly benefit from a mistake, and if he had made one, would have come to tell him about it, to explain what had happened.

So, he smiled.

"I haven't been under-assessed," he said.

"The figures here imply that you have, sir. They make it clear—" Cobb cleared his throat as if to prepare to sound even more impressive "—that you have claimed for expenses not met in the way of any business activity a total of twenty-seven thousand four hundred pounds, or a little under seven thousand each year. Allowance for the usual reliefs has already been made and the amount of income tax due on these sums is over three thousand pounds each year, or twelve thousand pounds."

Rollison was staring at him.

One part of his mind knew that no matter how serious this man was, there had been a mistake which would eventually be found out. The other part of his mind grappled with the fact that, so far as Cobb and this office was concerned, he had been adjudged an income tax evader on a substantial sum. And yet—and yet, *would* the authorities put this to him in such a way? If in fact they were convinced that he had fiddled the figures for four years, would they make some kind of charge? Would they simply add the arrears in this way and say nothing provided he paid up?

Cobb was still watching him very closely. Suspiciously? When Rollison simply sat and looked back at him, at least partly because he did not know what best to say, Cobb leaned forward and said in a deep voice: "I am quite sure that this should be regarded as an error, Mr. Rollison. You have claimed for expenses in connection with certain charitable activities, such as youth clubs, old folk's homes and similar no doubt worthy causes. However, these are not allowable. By adding the amount over-claimed for four years to the current year's assessment the Inspector has found the simplest way out. Don't you agree?"

Rollison began to frown, and then slowly, to smile. There was something here he did not understand but sooner or later he would, and for the time being it didn't really matter.

"No," answered Rollison, bluntly. "The simplest way is to find out why the agreement reached between my accountant and this office has suddenly been broken by the office. These charities, are in fact businesses. I do not in fact make a profit on them and incur a substantial loss but they are so designed that a profit *could* be made, so the losses are allowable. I'm sure that Mr. Slazenger will have to be consulted on this, there's no easy way to settle it between you and me. And, presumably, there is no hurry."

"Not for a week or so, certainly," Cobb conceded.

Rollison needed not a week or two but a month or two in New York, but he did not think this was the moment to say so. His smile broadened as he stood up from the rickety chair.

"I'll ask Mr. Slazenger to get in touch with you as soon as he's about again. Meanwhile, will you let me have details of the claims you previously allowed and now wish to disallow?" He stood with one hand outstretched, watching Cobb, who had one hand on his, Rollison's, file.

"I'll ask Mr. Watson to send them to you," Cobb promised. "These are only rough notes." He moved his hand towards Rollison's, his grasp firm and cool. "There is no need to go through the general office this time, this door leads straight to the passage." He moved towards the door which Rollison had used, and twisted the key. He seemed surprised when the lock didn't click, but turned the handle and opened the door wide.

"Goodbye, Mr. Rollison."

"Goodbye," Rollison said as he went out of the door.

Two things happened on the same instant. First, a gleam appeared in Cobb's eyes, as if he suddenly saw the funny side of this situation again: and second, as Rollison glanced along the passage, he saw a girl hurrying away, towards the landing. She wore a knee-length skirt and a short jacket; she had a nice figure and shiny dark hair. As she reached the landing she glanced back, then suddenly darted forward and disappeared down the stairs.

Rollison felt quite sure she had been listening at this doorway.

And he began to run, quite indifferent to what Cobb might think of his sudden change of pace.

Chapter 3

Pretty Girl

Rollison reached the corner as the lift arrived at the landing, but he did not wait for it, simply raced down the stairs, not caring how much noise he made above the footsteps of the fleeing girl. At the next landing he caught a glimpse of her skirt and heels. At the main lobby, he was within three feet of her. The lift had now reached the ground floor and a man was opening the gates. By using the stairs he had won perhaps five seconds.

The girl rushed out into the street, missed a shallow step, and began to fall. A middle-aged man, passing, shot out a hand to save her, and Rollison also shot out a hand. For a moment she was sandwiched between two arms.

"Sweetheart," Rollison said, "you really should look where you're going." He put his arm about her shoulders, firmly, and beamed at the other man. "Thank you very much, sir."

The man muttered: "S'all right," and went on. Rollison kept his arm round the girl's shoulders, looking down as she stared up at him. She had the look of a trapped creature, too frightened to move. Fear was a commonplace this morning.

This time, Rollison's smile was very warm and friendly and reassuring.

"Has anyone told you lately how very pretty you are?" he asked, and when she didn't answer he went on: "You really are, you know."

She managed to say: "Please—please let me go."

"But I need a talk with you."

"Please," she begged.

Slowly, he shook his head. She was as pretty as a picture, with violet eyes, glowing cheeks, a nice mouth and chin and a lovely complexion, and she was breathing hard, from running as well as from her fears.

"We must talk," he insisted.

"Oh, *please* let me go," she begged, almost in tears.

"As soon as you've told me why—" he began.

He saw her move and sensed what she was going to do, but could not dodge away in time. She kicked him on the shin, and it was like being struck by a pickaxe. Pain shot through him. He let her go and clenched his teeth, hardly knowing how to stop himself from crying out. The girl was trapped by parked cars, then pushed between two into the road and ran blindly.

Someone screamed.

Someone else cried out: "Oh, my God!"

Somehow, these cries pierced Rollison's anguish, and he opened his eyes and stared over the crowds, in time to hear the sickening thud of sound, to see the girl thrown into the air and then fall, spread-eagled over the front of the car, a small sports model painted dark green. The awful thing was that she was draped over it, a complete human being as far as one could see, but she must be smashed to nothing inside; she must be dead.

A woman was sobbing.

A man was calling: "Do something. For God's sake do something!"

Two others were moving slowly into the road. Some distance off, a policeman's helmet showed. Close by, a dozen cars were drawn up behind the sports car, which had slewed across the road. A driver at the back out of sight tooted on his horn. A man cried: "Stop that fool making a noise!" A woman from one of the cars got out as a man moved more briskly into the road; both were purposeful as they approached the sprawled body of the girl.

Pain still lanced through Rollison's left leg and spread upwards through his body.

The pointed shoe with which he had been kicked fell, slowly, from her foot to the roadway, and as it struck the smooth surface a red spot appeared near it. Just a small red spot; and another and another.

A youth suddenly collapsed against the side of a car, his face waxen-white.

A crowd had gathered, here and across the street; thirty, forty, fifty or more people, gaping. A motherly-looking woman bent over the youth. The woman from the car and the man from the pavement reached the girl and at last she was partly hidden from sight. What the older-looking man and woman did, Rollison could not tell.

The policeman was drawing near.

Rollison's pain had become less acute, was more a dull ache except at the spot where the girl had actually kicked him; at that point it throbbed and throbbed. He felt a trickle of something run down his leg, and realised that it was blood. He could see more blood on the road surface beneath the girl. The policeman was now with the man and woman, and the man said quite distinctly: "She's dead."

The hush was so great that the word sounded as if it were a trumpet call. "Dead, dead, dead." Someone said: "Oh, God." Two or three began to move on, glancing squeamishly towards the scene. An ambulance siren sounded: that had been very quick. Car engines started, too. A police car appeared from the other direction, and an officer got out and obviously began to judge the distance between the sports car and the nearest car parked against the kerb. There was a consultation, before two of the police and two spectators lifted a parked car a foot closer to the kerb, so that there was room to pass.

Cars crawled by.

The ambulance drew up, and ambulance men jumped down.

A man was saying: "Ghastly. Absolutely ghastly."

The youth who had fainted began to retch, and the motherly woman said tenderly: "Now, now, you'll be all right."

All this time, Rollison had stood with one foot raised off the ground, a hand on the wall, to support him. And while he had observed everything, one thing had held his attention more than any other, and one thing had appalled him. Others were staring as if they realised it, too.

The driver of the sports car hadn't moved. He hadn't shown his face, hadn't attempted to open the door. He sat back in his seat, one arm draped over the wheel. His tweed cap was set at a rakish angle over his right eye and covered most of his forehead and cheek; he had a pointed nose and a long and pointed chin.

But this, which held Rollison's attention most, was nothing compared with the appalling fact: *he himself had sent that girl to her death*. The phrase repeated itself over and over in his mind. *He had sent that girl to her death*. She still seemed in front of him, so pretty and charming, and pleading. "Please—please let me go." And after a moment: "Please." And when he had said that they must talk, there had been such anguish in her: "Oh, *please* let me go."

She had at last pulled herself away as if in a blind panic.

Had he released her earlier or held on to her more tightly, she would be alive now. *Alive*. Breathing. Unbroken. Instead—

The policemen and some of the passers-by had formed a cordon about the front of the sports car, and the ambulance men were moving the girl. A stretcher lay on the road, waiting. The woman who had gone to the car said in her clear, carrying voice: "It was instantaneous. Quite instantaneous."

"You see, love," the motherly woman tried to reassure her newfound charge, "she didn't feel a thing. Not a thing. You don't want to take on so."

People began to move and talk, saying all the commonplace things, of how terrible it was, ghastly, horrible, poor thing, terrible...

Policemen began to move about the people, asking questions. The remarkable thing was that the crowd began to thin out at once, only a few who had arrived after the impact lingered, and their voices made a refrain. "I didn't see what happened ... I didn't see a thing ... I didn't come until later ... I didn't see a thing." The body was lifted into the ambulance, two of the men climbed in with it and the ambulance moved off. Traffic was now moving past the sports car, where two policemen were standing, hiding the driver from Rollison. The crowd was now drifting in all directions. Rollison moved his leg up and down, finding it very painful. He looked down, to find blood soaking his sock. He turned his back on the road and placed the foot of his injured leg on the step the girl had slipped on.

Alive.

He pulled up the leg of his trousers, and pursed his lips. There was a nasty little cut which had bled freely, and two streams of blood, coagulating at the edges, rolled down to the sock. He must get home and clean this up.

A man exclaimed: "Mr. Rollison!"

He turned round, to see a youthful policeman looking up at him, a pleasant-faced youth whose tall helmet simply served to emphasise how short he was.

"Hallo," Rollison said.

"I thought I recognised you, sir! Did you by any chance see the accident just now?"

"Yes," answered Rollison. "I did."

The policeman's eyes lit up as Rollison began to wonder just how much he should say. That the girl had been upstairs, listening at the Inspector's keyhole? That he had chased her down the stairs, held her back, rejected her pleading? The youth took out a notebook.

"Just what *did* happen, sir?"

Rollison said slowly: "I was behind her, on these steps. She slipped. A man was passing and he and I saved her from falling." He noticed the policeman was using shorthand and seemed to have no difficulty in keeping up with what he was saying. "When I let her go she turned and ran into the road."

"*Ran,* sir?"

"Yes."

"Why, sir?"

"I don't know," Rollison replied.

"Was there anyone following her?" asked the policeman.

"Not to my knowledge," Rollison said.

"Did you *see* anyone chasing after her?"

"No."

"But she ran?"

"People are sometimes in a hurry," Rollison pointed out drily. "You don't have to be scared out of your wits to run across the road." But she had been terrified and he had terrified her.

"No, sir. Quite so. Was she alone, sir?"

"Yes."

"Did you know her, by any chance?"

"No," Rollison answered. "I had never seen her before."

The policeman folded his notebook and tucked it behind the small transistor radio already in his pocket, then said earnestly: "I'm very grateful. You do understand that you may be called to give testimony at the inquest, don't you?"

"Yes," Rollison said bleakly.

"Silly question to ask you," the young man admitted. He gave a kind of salute, then turned and walked towards a sergeant who was talking to a small group of people. He saw a taxi approaching, its hire sign alight, and waved to it. Soon, he was sitting back in a corner of the cab, feeling hot and cold in turn. He lit a cigarette, and placed the match carefully in an ashtray.

He shivered convulsively.

It would be a long time before he forgot the sight and sound of the 'accident'.

He muttered: "But for me, she would be alive."

That was both true and false, and he began to argue with himself, which was a good sign: he was recovering. He pulled up the trouser leg again, and tied a handkerchief round the calf, covering the wound and soaking up some of the blood.

He hadn't made the girl act as eavesdropper, and if she hadn't been outside that door and guilty enough to run away she would still be alive. He had done the obvious thing; at least, the obvious and almost inevitable thing for him. He had wanted to know, *needed* to know, why she had been so intent at that keyhole. He hadn't had any choice. Moreover, he had not bullied or struck her. In fact he had been pleasant; even amiable. She had been frightened because she had been caught, and that meant she had been frightened of someone else or else frightened of the consequences of what she had done.

That 'someone else' was the real cause of her death.

"Very rational," he announced aloud. "I suppose it's true and convincing, too. But—" He broke off, without uttering his thoughts, which were simply: If I hadn't grabbed her and held on, she would probably still be alive. If I'd held on to her, she would be.

The taxi swung too fast round a corner and Rollison had to cling to the safety strap to save himself from being flung against the other door. This was a day for accidents! Where was he? This was the corner of Piccadilly and Brook Street, he would soon be at Gresham Terrace, where he lived in the top flat of Number 25, known to his friends and the postal service as *25g, Gresham Terrace, London, W.1.* He took a seven-sided fifty-pence piece from his pocket, a coin once hated but now quite popular, and handed it to the driver as they drew up outside the house.

Gresham Terrace was its normal self.

Apart from the rasp of the taxi engine and an echo of the driver's 'Thank you, sir', there was little sound. A faint squeak sounded a few yards away, as a nursemaid pushed a baby carriage. The purring of a Rolls-Royce as an acquaintance of Rollison drove by. The sharp tapping of a woman's feet, heels protected by iron tips.

The dead girl's heels had been of rubber; otherwise she would have made much more sound.

He didn't even know her name!

He unlocked the front door and stepped into the wide passage which led up a flight of stone but warmly carpeted stairs; the carpet was new. As he closed the door, the hall and staircase seemed to go dark. His heart dropped as he stepped on to the bottom stair and fresh pain shot through his injured leg. There were four flights to *go,* and no lift. What on earth made him live at the top of a house where there was no lift? Habit? It certainly wasn't convenience, and on this particular walk up every step hurt, until on the top flight he was glad of the handrail, both for support and for help in getting up.

He was at the half-landing beneath his flat, with only a short half-flight to go when the door opened and a man appeared, while the voice of Jolly, his – the Toff's – man sounded clearly.

"I will tell Mr. Rollison the moment he arrives, sir."

Then the man who was leaving turned, and Rollison saw that it was old friend and yet old adversary, the man he knew better than any human being except his friend and factotum, Jolly.

Superintendent William Grice, a senior detective at New Scotland

Yard, turned and looked down at him; there was no pleasure, only sternness, in his gaze.

Chapter 4

Superintendent Grice

Rollison, caught on the bottom step and gripping the handrail tightly, returned the Yard man's stare without his customary pleasure, too. All he wanted to do was get into his flat and have the leg bathed. The proper salve would not only heal the 'wound' but would greatly reduce the pain. An hour's rest would take away the slight nausea which lingered in his stomach and the headache which had started at the back of his head and spread until it was everywhere, particularly behind the eyes.

The last thing he needed was a meeting with Grice in his present mood.

Grice said in a voice as disapproving as his expression: "So you're back."

"With luck I might even reach the top of the stairs," Rollison replied, and flexed the muscles of his left arm and put his good leg on the next step.

Grice frowned in puzzlement as Rollison climbed three steps this way, then came to rest. During the seconds which passed concern drove the other emotions from Grice's face while Jolly, until then hidden from the Toff, moved forward, rounded Grice and hurried down the stairs. He did not speak, simply ranged himself on Rollison's side, facing upwards, and steadied rather than supported him. Rollison had to make an effort with each step, but as he reached the top where Grice now stood in the front doorway, he essayed a smile; and it was bright and friendly, as if sight of Grice had for the moment driven pain away.

"Hallo, Bill," he said lightly. "A friend in need is a friend indeed, don't they say?" He sounded inane, as he often did when making an effort to hide his feelings.

"What's happened to you?" demanded Grice.

"I was hacked on the shin."

"Hacked?"

"Kicked. And" – he had to grit his teeth before he could retain the light note while saying – "to make it worse, by a pretty young woman."

"Then no doubt you asked for it," Grice growled.

"If I may say so, sir, that remark was most uncalled for," said Jolly. He gave Grice a long and reproachful glance, and Grice at least had the grace to colour slightly and to turn back into the hall-cum-lounge behind him. "Are you able to walk to the bathroom, sir? Or would you prefer to sit in the study or lie on your bed?" The tone of Jolly's voice changed to obvious concern.

"The bathroom, I think," Rollison decided. "And then some tea and aspirins." His look at Grice was friendly enough but not facetious. "It was a hell of a kick and a hell of a situation, and I don't feel very good."

"I can see you don't," Grice said, with some sympathy. "Can I help?"

There was a brief pause as Jolly closed the door behind them; then Jolly conceded that was a concession indeed; a declaration of peace.

"If you would be good enough to put the kettle on for tea, sir, I would be grateful."

Grice turned away and disappeared along a passage which was nearly opposite the entrance door. Not far along the passage was the kitchen, usually prohibited to all but Jolly and a few accepted domestics.

Jolly and Rollison followed at a slower gait.

Rollison was so annoyed with himself for feeling so bad from a girl's kick, and curious about Grice's presence, that it did not occur to him that, now he was in the flat, all the reasons for his staying here were evident. Apart from the fact that it was in the heart of Mayfair and so close to all the best cultural facilities, the flat itself was large and intelligently arranged. The one passage led not only to the domestic quarters including Jolly's bed and bathroom, but also to a cloakroom. At the far end was another passage, leading right, to the main cloakroom and spare bedroom, each with its own bath; and this passage opened into the study-cum-living room, with a raised dining alcove at one end and windows opposite, across the large room. There was a second entrance to this room from the lounge-hall.

All of this was furnished with masculine elegance, yet a woman could feel at home here; and some did.

The shortest way to Rollison's room was along the passage where Grice had gone. Very soon, Rollison was in his own bathroom, sitting on a stool, and Jolly was looking down at the wound.

"That is very nasty, sir."

"Hardly crippling, though," Rollison grumbled.

"It caught a vein and the shin, sir, and—" Jolly broke off and busied himself with a bowl of water placed beneath Rollison's outstretched leg, a sponge, an antiseptic which was as pungent as it was powerful.

Jolly was both gentle and firm, yet his ministrations were painful. It was easy to see why. The kick, obviously delivered with great force, had not only cut but lifted the skin and what little flesh there was between skin and shin, for at least two inches, leaving it raw and ugly-looking. Jolly cleaned and had it ready for a salve before removing Rollison's blood-soaked shoe and sock. Grice came in and watched, and as Jolly washed the dried blood, the detective observed: "She seems to have known how to kick."

"Yes," Rollison said bleakly. "Yes indeed."

"Where did it happen?" Grice asked, obviously checking himself from adding: "And why?"

"In Pleydell Street," stated Rollison, watching Grice closely.

Grice was taken right off his balance. He even leaned against the airing cupboard at the end of the bath, pursing his lips. He was over six feet tall, a broad-shouldered, lean-hipped, sparely-built man with no excess flesh. His face was aquiline, the nose slightly hooked and the skin stretched so tight at the bridge that it was almost white, although he had an olive skin which always looked sunburned. He had brown eyes, clearly defined lips, and on the left side of his face a burn scar; he had been burned when a bomb intended for the Toff had exploded as he examined it.

That had really been the beginning of their friendship.

Jolly, standing up from his labours, looked seventy but was in fact in his early sixties. He had a very lined face, a sad, at times doleful, some said dyspeptic, expression. Beneath his chin the skin sagged, like that of a man who had once been heavy-jowled and had lost weight on a crash diet. In the way of Watson! His eyes, too, were brown, the lids were wrinkled. He had thinning grey hair and a small bald spot.

"In Pleydell Street," Grice said at last. "So you admit it."

"I state it," corrected Rollison.

"Rolly," Grice said in a voice obviously schooled to sound friendly. "When I saw a police constable's report that you'd been there I came round at once, hoping he was wrong. When are you going to stop playing the fool?"

"I didn't know I had played the fool lately."

"Then what the hell do you think you're doing now?" Grice exploded.

Jolly finished spreading a salve over the clean-looking wound, and picked up a box of adhesive plasters. He shot Grice a disapproving look, then selected a large plaster, big enough to cover the skinned patch. Rollison, meanwhile, returned Grice's angry glare with a blank look, and slowly shook his head.

"Can't you see?" he demanded.

"For God's sake don't make light of it! This affair could be deadly."

It began to dawn on Rollison that Grice was not simply trying to upset him or to make him talk: he was acutely distressed. For the first time since he had reached here, Rollison began to be able to think. Until then he had been so oppressed by the mental image of what had happened and by the pain; now, he slipped back into his real self, saw how worried Grice was, knew something very serious was troubling him.

He said: "Yes, Bill. I've found that out already."

"Why the hell didn't you tell me what you knew and what you were planning?"

Rollison said: "Because I wasn't planning a thing and didn't know a thing."

Grice's lips parted, he looked about to shout: "Don't lie to me!" But he bit back the words. Rollison put a hand on Jolly's shoulder and eased himself up, aware that Jolly was now staring at him in puzzlement; Jolly, clearly, had been too concerned with the injured leg to think seriously about Grice's manner; but Jolly was seldom befuddled or preoccupied for long.

"Make the tea, will you?" Rollison asked him. "Mr. Grice will stop me from collapsing." He tested his leg. "That's much better. I didn't know I could make such a fuss about a trifle." He waved Jolly out of the bathroom and Grice led him by the short passage into the big room. Trifle or not, he still had to walk with care. He went to a large armchair which faced the passage and grunted as he sat down. Grice pushed up a leather-covered pouffe.

"Thanks."

"Pleasure. Will you now tell me what happened?"

"If you will (a) stop jumping down my throat, and (b) assume I am telling the truth and not trying to deceive you."

Grice grunted: "That will be the day."

"It has to be the day. I'm neither in mood nor shape to have a shouting match or a game of cat and mouse with you. Or for that matter, with anybody."

"What's upset you so?" demanded Grice. He sat on a corner of a large, flat-topped desk, gripping the edge with his hands. His back was to a high wall which had remarkable miscellany of objects on it, most of them weapons. This was called the Trophy Wall and each trophy or exhibit was a memento of a case in which the Toff had been involved. These two men were perhaps the least impressed of any in the world with the remarkable tales the Trophy Wall told.

Rollison said briskly: "I shall make it as brief as I can." He paused, pursing his lips. "I am planning to go to America, to spend a few romantic weeks with Chellis Spiro. I thought I'd cleared everything up. Out of the blue came a demand for double my usual income tax, a sum large enough to hurt. My accountant is ill with a slipped disc. After a chat with him I went to see the taxman myself. I saw him. He was terrified."

All this time, Rollison had been studying Grice closely, and had observed the changing emotions which crossed the detective's alert face. First, a kind of stubborn determination to listen patiently. Next, astonishment. Next, no doubt, incredulity, although the fact that the Toff was clearing the decks for a visit to the United States must surely have convinced him that this story was literally true.

After the incredulity there came almost baffled amazement which ended with open-mouthed astonishment when Rollison stated so starkly: "He was terrified."

Now, Rollison's pause invited Grice to put questions, and with great deliberation, he asked: "What terrified him?"

"At least one thing I don't know about. And certainly, I did."

"Then you *did* go to put the fear of God into him!" Grice burst out.

"No, Bill," Rollison replied gently. "I don't know why he was scared out of his wits of me, but he was." He leaned back and closed his eyes. "Not all the time, mind you."

Jolly came in with a laden tray; not only tea but coffee, not only milk but cream, not only biscuits but wafer-thin sandwiches. He placed this on a knee-high table near the Toff, a Scandinavian contemporary piece which merged with the older pieces ranging from a William and Mary oyster-shell cabinet in walnut to a Regency writing desk known to the initiated as an escritoire. As he poured out, coffee for Grice, tea for Rollison, Rollison asked: "Did you get the gist of what I've told Mr. Grice, Jolly?"

"Yes, sir." Jolly had a microphone in the kitchen which could pick up what was being said anywhere in the flat; there were several such microphones here. There was a tacit understanding between them about the occasions when Jolly should listen in; and he always chose the right occasion.

"Then I'll go straight on. Sit down, Jolly." Jolly chose a small armchair and sank back into it, while Grice continued to sit against the desk, cup and saucer in hand, a plate with sandwiches where his right hand had been. "The Inspector of Taxes, a Mr. F. Watson, was alarmed by something but amiable enough when I first arrived. And his staff descended on me for autographs. Then Watson had a telephone call, and real terror struck."

"Have you any idea what caused it?" asked Grice.

"I only know that he seemed to see me as the Devil in modern dress, and grabbed the first excuse he could to get away. I suspect that he told one of his staff to fake a summons to his head office in Whitehall, and he rushed off. He was replaced by a deputy, name Cobb. Cobb accused me of making false income tax returns."

"Good Lord!" exclaimed Grice.

"How absurd can officialdom get?" demanded Jolly, indignantly.

"Had he any evidence?" demanded Grice, as if eagerly.

"He wouldn't show me all he had but promised to write with full details," Rollison answered, briskly. He drank more tea and bit off a piece of a shortcake biscuit before going on: "He let me out of the office by a side door. A girl who had been eavesdropping there cut and run for it. I had never seen her before, and gave chase. I caught her as she stepped, in fact nearly fell, into Pleydell Street. She asked me – pleaded with me – to let her go. I held on to her, saying we needed to talk. She kicked me on the shin and got free and ran straight into the path of a car. She must have died instantly," Rollison gulped. "It was not a good thing to see."

When he stopped, there was a deep silence; even a profound one. Grice put his cup down and stood up. Jolly sat against the back of his chair, obviously deeply troubled. Rollison finished his biscuit and Jolly sprang forward to give him some more tea.

"It must have been a most disturbing experience," he remarked.

"Very disturbing," Rollison agreed. "If I had let her go at once she would probably have gone along the street, not across it. And she wouldn't have been in such a blind panic. If I'd held on to her she would still be alive." His thoughts stirred. "She *was* in panic and the Inspector of Taxes *was* in terror, all because of me."

"And you don't know why?" Grice again seemed to breathe scepticism.

"I don't know why."

"Your tea," said Jolly.

"All I know and cannot emphasise too much," said Rollison, taking the cup and saucer, "is that if I had let her go earlier or if I had held on to her, she would be alive now. So in a way, I killed her." He turned and looked intently into Grice's eyes and went on in a steely voice: "I know no more than I've told you, Bill. I had no prior knowledge of the affair, but from this moment on it is my business. Avenging the girl is my business. I'll work with the police or without them, and if I have to in spite of them, but I shall work to find out who killed her, and bring the murderer to book."

As he finished, he looked defiantly into Grice's eyes, as if expecting to be warned off at once. But Grice did not warn him off. He stood up, put his cup and saucer back on the tray, looked down at the Toff and replied very quietly.

"It must be with us, Rolly. I know nothing would make you hold off and there's no sense in cutting each other's throats." He paused, only to go on: "We want to find the truth as much as you do. Watson is the third Inspector of Income Tax in the Central London area known to be frightened out of his wits. Members of their staffs have reported this, but so far we don't know what the cause is." He paused but held a hand out, discouraging the others from making comment. He seemed to be assessing his thoughts very carefully before he went on: "I heard you had been an eyewitness and assumed you were already in the hunt. For what it's worth, I'm sorry." Rollison waved a hand as if to say "Forget it", and Grice went on very quietly: "Did you notice the driver of the car involved, Rolly?"

Rollison's throat went dry.

"Yes," he answered. "A young man."

"He also died," Grice told him. "It seems of a heart attack."

Chapter 5

Two to Avenge

The shadow which had lifted from Rollison for a few moments in the telling of the story, once more gathered about him, dark as a threatening storm. There was no sound but their breathing; not even Jolly stirred. Rollison seemed to be lifted out of this room to the entrance to the office building in Pleydell Street; had a vivid mental picture of the girl's body draped, lifeless, over the front of the car, and the young man so improbably upright at the steering wheel. He felt as if he would never be able to get either sight out of his mind. He could even feel the pain from that savage kick; it was as if he had really gone back in time.

Slowly, the tension faded, relief and a kind of pleasure replaced it. Grice of course believed him, and had immediately conceded that they must work together. The time when he had relished a running battle with crooks on one side and the police on the other, had long gone – even if, in emergency, he would still wage such a fight.

At last, Jolly spoke.

"Is there anything else you need, sir?"

"No," Rollison said.

Jolly stood up and collected cups and saucers and plates and put them on the tray. He would switch on his loudspeaker as soon as he reached the kitchen, and the more he knew the better when the Toff came to discuss the case with him.

Grice took the seat Jolly had been in.

"Rolly," he said.

"Yes?"

"Had you played the fool over income tax?"

"No."

"The most unexpected people do, you know."

"So I've been told."

"One of the senior superintendents at the Yard had been receiving payment for books he wrote under a pen name and didn't declare the income."

"What a bad man he must have been!"

Grice ignored the attempt at flippancy, and went on: "Few people seem to think it a real crime to cheat income tax or customs. You must know that. There seem to be double standards of honesty in most people on these things."

"I do know."

"And you haven't played the fool?"

"I have not," asserted Rollison.

Yet he had a feeling that Grice was not fully satisfied; that the other averted his gaze because of his doubts. Moreover it was very true that the most upright of people, who would not cheat a human being of a penny, would not cheat on public transport or in any form of business, who would find a richly-filled purse or wallet and take it to the nearest police station, would try to walk through customs adorned with wristwatches, diamond rings, fur coats or carrying currency; and they would lie until they were black in the face in their income tax returns.

"You know," Grice said. "I've had a lot of investigation to do into income tax evasion, with the tax people. I was in charge of a case only a few months ago which involved a peer of the realm, and another involving a well-known politician."

"I no doubt should be astounded," remarked the Toff, drily.

Grice appeared not to notice that remark, and went on musingly: "The tax people appear to have evolved a method to fight it. They appear to work on the principle that everything a man or woman earns shows up sooner or later. Instead of making a big song and dance about it, they simply add the total to the latest assessment. More often than not the taxpayer takes a deep breath and swallows the bitter dose. Occasionally, one denies everything, and there has to be a full investigation in which we at the Yard help. Now and again a mistake is proved, but that generally comes out before a case is taken to court. If there's obvious intent to defraud or to avoid payment it's always taken to court."

Rollison did not comment.

"This way the State gets its due and the individual saves face," Grice went on.

"And, possibly, goes bankrupt," put in Rollison, coldly.

"Seldom," Grice said.

"Too often," Rollison argued.

"Possibly," Grice conceded, "but the law's the law, Rolly. I might not like some aspects of it, but I have to enforce it and so in their way do the tax people." Grice was no longer musing but being very earnest, even intent. "The only way to fight tax is through political channels. Which reminds me: are you going to continue with politics?"

"No."

"That seems very definite."

"It is," declared Rollison.

"I don't know whether to be pleased or sorry," replied Grice, giving a grim smile. "If you were lashing about you in politics you would have little time to investigate crime."

"And think of the criminals who would wallow in freedom and luxury then," retorted the Toff.

This exchange helped him; lifted the shadow and lightened the burden. And there was the familiar camaraderie with Grace, they were discussing rather than arguing. He felt much more at ease.

"Think how many more we would have time to catch if we didn't have to spend so much time with you," Grice riposted. That obviously put him in a good mood, so that he spoke even more naturally and went on without affronting the Toff. "I was saying, whether we like the rate of income and surtax or not, we have to live with it and any new method of getting unpaid taxes without causing delinquents a lot of shame as well as money seems a good one to me."

"Do you mean to say—" began Rollison, obviously horrified.

"Good Lord, it's not *official!*" exclaimed Grice. "It's simply a system adopted by more and more Inspectors of Taxes. I doubt if there is even an unwritten law about it. More likely there's a kind of grapevine which links all the Inspectors of Revenue and the rule seems to be: *Get as much as you can with as little fuss as you can.* And Rolly – it works."

"I'm not at all sure it isn't a form of whitemail," Rollison objected.

"Nonsense! Finding a way of making a man pay his just dues isn't white or blackmail. What's got into you? It's the kind of thing you should want to do yourself!" Grice actually laughed; a kind of chortle. "The point I am making is that velvet glove methods often work where iron hand tactics fail."

"I have taken your point," Rollison said, with affected coldness. "If I admit to my sins, I will simply pay up – and that will be considered sufficient punishment."

"Precisely," agreed Grice.

"But in matters of tax I've committed no sins," Rollison asserted.

"Then you're a rare bird," replied Grice. "For sin, read 'mistake' or 'oversight' and think again."

"I have thought and thought," Rollison replied earnestly. "And if they don't drop it I shall fight and fight – even to the doors of the bankruptcy court."

They stared at each other, long and appraisingly, as if each was trying to make sure whether the other meant what he said or not. No one, watching, could have doubted that they each did.

Grice shifted first.

"Don't say I didn't warn you," he said laconically. "Now, other things."

"Bill—" Rollison began, and paused.

"Yes?"

"Did you say three Inspectors of Income Tax are known to be scared?"

"Yes."

"Really in trouble?"

"Yes. They are very nervous, sleep badly, scare easily, and generally behave as if they were having the wits scared out of them."

"Have you the slightest idea why?"

"Not yet."

"Haven't they talked? Hasn't even one of them talked?"

"Not one."

"How do you know they're terrified?"

"Some member of their staff has reported it to V.I.P.'s and we've been asked to check with the wives concerned. The wives aren't eager to discuss it but there isn't any doubt, Rolly – these men are scared."

"Do you have any ideas?" asked Rollison quietly.

"Ideas, yes. Knowledge, no."

"You couldn't share your ideas, could you?"

"Why don't you make an intelligent deduction," countered Grice.

"Very well," said the Toff, and paused and pondered, more to marshal his words than to extract an idea from his mind. He still felt more relaxed, and knew that one reason was that he had been given a go-ahead to investigate the death of the girl. There was more. She had been eavesdropping; whatever she heard should have been reported to whoever had sent her there. Of course she might possibly have been working in her own interests but Rollison felt it much more likely that she had been acting for some third party.

Why?

Could anyone want to find out whether he, the Toff, had been trying to cheat the taxman; or more accurately, the country?

He put that question aside, sure that sooner or later the answer would come, and began to reply to Grice with 'intelligent deduction'.

"If some people or companies have been caught in a fiddle, they might think it worthwhile making the taxman keep quiet. Some might bribe or otherwise try to persuade a taxman to destroy any evidence he'd collected, and if bribery failed, might try to frighten him into it. So any one of the terrified taxmen may have unearthed a guilty secret which hasn't yet been brought into the open. The Inspector's authority in his own office is pretty complete, and it shouldn't be too difficult to keep the details from his staff even if his manner gave him away."

He finished, and sat back, ready for Grice's reaction.

"Very intelligent," Grice said. "That could be the answer, Rolly."

"And you've no idea who the terrifying taxpayer might be?"

"Not yet," admitted Grice.

"Have you been officially consulted, do you say?"

"Good God, yes!"

"You don't have to be so indignant about it," murmured Rollison. "Well, I haven't been even unofficially consulted and I haven't the slightest idea why the girl should have been so interested in my tax problems, or the Inspector."

Other things were drifting into his mind. The fact that he had sent Johnny P. Rains after Watson for instance. The fact that someone must have scared Watson about his, the Toff's, visit while they had been sitting together. The fact that Cobb's manner had been so strange and changeable. He had told Grice of none of these things, and the fact of using Johnny P. Rains was one which Grice would undoubtedly consider important. Rollison actually contemplated telling him and the story was on the tip of his tongue when the telephone bell rang. Almost at once it ceased ringing, Jolly had taken the call on his extension. Very soon he came into the room, saying: "The call is for Mr. Grice, sir."

Grice sprang to his feet, a man of surprising speed and ease of movement, and went to the desk. Jolly asked Rollison a silent question with a raise of his eyebrows. The question was: "Shall I listen in?" Rollison shook his head, and in any case there wasn't time, for Grice said: "I'll be over at once," and replaced the receiver. "I have to go back to the Yard," he said. "There's some doubt about whether that driver *did* die of a heart attack." Already Grice was heading for the lounge-hall and Jolly was trying to reach and open the door before him. "You won't be going out, will you, Rolly?"

"Not if I can help it."

"I'll call you if there's any news of importance," Grice promised, and went off as Jolly opened the door.

In a way, it was like watching a whirlwind.

Something had changed recently in Grice, Rollison thought: he had seldom been a man of such swift movement, rather a slow and deliberate man who liked to think before he decided what action to take. The reason seemed not to matter, but a 'new' Grice would have to be watched.

He sat back. Chair and stool were very comfortable and the pain had gone from his leg, leaving only a dull ache. His head still ached, but not so severely, although Jolly had forgotten the aspirins; it was rare for Jolly to forget. It was rare for him to go to his own quarters instead of, quietly agog, to the study when there was so much to discuss. He was soon on his way, however, and he carried a tray with some tablets and a glass of water.

"I thought it would be better if you had these tablets after Mr. Grice had left," he said. "It will be much easier for you to relax now, and they will do you much more good." He shook two of a brand of aspirins on to a saucer as he went on: "Have you any specific instructions for me, sir, before you take these?"

Rollison put his head on one side and studied his man for what seemed a long time before he said: "Yes. Remind me, if I ever show signs of forgetting, that I owe you much more than I shall ever be able to say."

Jolly, taken completely by surprise, stood with the small tray on one hand and his gaze on the Toff; and very slowly he turned a dusky, near-purply red. Slowly, he recovered. Once he tried to speak but managed only a croak; the second time he simply sounded husky.

"You—you are no more likely to forget than I am likely to forget how true it is of you to me, sir." His gaze was very direct, his colour gradually receded, and he relaxed, picking up the saucer.

"A man named Johnny P. Rains was to do a job for me," Rollison said. "If he comes or telephones I want to talk to him. If anyone else calls, use your own judgment whether to disturb me." The telephone in this room could be switched through to Jolly's apartments if need be, leaving Rollison undisturbed.

"Johnny P. Rains," repeated Jolly. "I seem to remember the name, sir. Isn't he a private enquiry agent?" He nodded when Rollison said 'yes'. Rollison took the tablets and settled back gratefully in the armchair. He knew quite well that he was suffering from shock, and needed a few hours of quiet; and that Jolly was determined he should get them. Chair and stool and head-cushion were comfortable, and Rollison was slightly oblique to the Trophy Wall. Drowsily, he recollected some of the cases. The early one in Limehouse when the old boot hanging there had nearly killed him. The top hat with the hole in it, a hole made by a bullet which had knocked it off Rollison's head and taken off some of his then jet black hair. The silk stocking which had been used to strangle two girls – or was it three? – the chicken feathers plucked from a fowl cooked and poisoned for his dinner.

There were so many of them; each a trophy, he reminded himself, of a case in which he and Jolly had brought a criminal or more to book.

But this was the first case which had involved a taxman.

Then he was reminded of his own supposed fraud, and for a moment was very indignant indeed. But he drowsed off; even thought of the girl did not prevent it, and he was sure Jolly had given him tablets much stronger than aspirins.

Jolly was probably wise, if he had.

Rollison's last waking thought was that he did not even know the girl's name.

Chapter 6

Daisy and Violet

Her name was Daisy Bell. They found it in a driving licence in her handbag. Her address was 25, Quaker Street, Whitechapel. She had four photographs in a small wallet, one hundred and eighteen pounds in a side pocket of her handbag, and a pound's worth of change. The photographs were laid out on a table in a room at the hospital where the body lay. Death had yet to be certified; only when it was could Daisy Bell be taken to the morgue at the nearby police station.

A tall, gangling young man, Detective Sergeant Moriarty, and a very heavy and thick-set older man, Detective Officer Odlum, arrived at the Charing Cross hospital to see the girl and everything she had in her purse and on her clothing. This was while Grice was at Rollison's flat. They were already assigned to the income tax enquiries, and had been sent here because this girl – or one very like her – had been seen before at the two other income tax offices where there were frightened inspectors. It was Odlum, who had piggy little eyes and a rosebud mouth, who stared down at the photographs. Moriarty was at the bedside, looking at the girl's face, which had hardly a scratch or a bruise.

"Sergeant," Odlum called.

Moriarty walked towards him.

Moriarty had a slightly negroid look, although his skin was white. He had very curly, wiry hair and startled-looking eyes, not at all what a policeman might be expected to look like. He said "What is it, mate?" in the broadest of Cockney, and looked down at the photographs. Odlum stared sideways at him, as he breathed: "Gawd."

"How about that?" asked Odlum.

"It's bloody uncanny," Moriarty declared.

"Uncanny is the word."

Moriarty picked up two of the photographs, each of which was of a young girl. The girls could have been identical but for one thing; one photographed face had a scar, on the forehead and the side of the cheek, the other face was without blemish. Moriarty carried these to the bed and looked at the photographs, then back to the dead girl.

"Twins, I should think," he declared.

"The spitting image," agreed Odium. "Anything on the back?"

There *was* something on the back: a pencilled name and date. On the one with the scar was the name Violet, and on the unblemished one, Daisy. The date on each was the same: *3rd September, 1972.* Moriarty pursed his full lips, and put the photographs back, then took out some small plastic bags and began to put a photograph into one. Between them the policemen, almost indifferently, sealed each bag and marked details of the contents on a small tie-on tag.

Soon, the job was done.

Soon, a young doctor came in and tested pulse and heart and eyes and lungs, and pronounced poor Daisy Bell dead. The policeman left before she was removed, and telephoned the Yard. The Inspector who took the message passed it on to a Superintendent who was waiting with the information when Grice returned from seeing Rollison. Almost at once, Grice asked: "Has anyone looked for the parents yet?"

For the other photographs were of a man and a woman, each looking about fifty; and the woman in particular was very like the girls.

"Not as far as I know," the other man said.

"I'll talk to Division," Grice promised.

No one liked the task of telling relatives of sudden death. There was a theory that the police were hardened to this and to much else, but only a few were truly indifferent. The Superintendent in charge at Whitechapel would know whom to send to the parents, or the sister, and Grice put in a call to him. His name was Smith; Grice knew him as a big, husky, hearty man with a hoarse voice.

Smith listened.

"*What* was the name?" he demanded; obviously he did not like this news at all.

"Bell," Grice said, and felt it was a name out of a songbook rather than life. "Daisy Bell."

Smith did not answer at once, and Grice could picture him with his badly shaven face and hairs at his nostrils and ears; a ruddy, rather sandy-looking man.

"With a sister named Violet," he said at last.

"Yes. What's worrying you about this couple, Smithy? Worrying you more than usual, I mean?"

"Plenty," answered Smith. "You wouldn't remember, would you, the name of Ding Dong Bell?"

"*Ding* Dong Bell!" exclaimed Grice.

"So you do remember."

"Yes," Grice said, gulping. "I remember. He went down for ten years for robbery with violence – *how* long ago?"

"Twenty years," answered Smith. "He's been out for twelve years, earned full remission. We've never got him for anything else since but he hates every bloody copper he ever sets eyes on. Tell you one thing, Bill. We haven't got a man in the division who could do this job the way it ought to be done. Those Bells are one big happy family. I don't know why for certain, but after Ding Dong went inside Big Daisy his wife worked her fingers to the bone looking after those kids." Smith was waxing, for him, quite poetic, obviously to cover his feelings. Then abruptly, he said: "Bill, I don't like it."

Grice asked, obtusely: "What in particular?"

"Ding Dong will go berserk. Absolutely berserk. He did once before, when Violet was cut up about the face."

"*Cut?*" breathed Grice.

"She was attacked with a razor." There was an audible gulp from the other end of the line. "And the chap who did it was killed in a car accident a year later. *I* never thought that was really an accident.

Bill, you can take it from me that this could lead to real trouble. We've got to handle it as if it was red-hot."

"It was red-hot before I knew this," Grice said grimly. "Well, berserk or not, Ding Dong has got to be told. Will you do it yourself?"

Smith said heavily: "If I must. I've been thinking, though. This *was* an accident, wasn't it? I mean, she wasn't running from our chaps?"

"No."

"Then we don't have to show we're so interested in her. And I know a man I'd rather have tell Ding Dong," said Smith. "Someone who'll keep him quiet if anyone can. You know the chap I've got in mind, he'll do it if we put it to him nicely. And he'll know the need for it, Ding Dong's a regular at the Blue Dog."

"Are you talking about Bill Ebbutt?" Grice demanded, suddenly shrill.

"That's the man," confirmed Smith. "No reason against it, have you?"

Slowly, Grice said: "No. No, I suppose not." But he shivered, for the real significance of what he had heard was only now coming home to him. It seemed a long time before he spoke again, and then it was in his usual decisive voice: the voice of authority. "Yes, I have," he decided.

"This is a job we must do ourselves. I think I'll come over myself. Expect me in an hour's time."

"But *why?*" Smith roared.

"I'll tell you when I see you," Grice promised, and put down the receiver.

He wished he could talk to Rollison but decided it would be better to allow him to rest; in any case Jolly would see that he did. Jolly knew as well as Grice that the sight of the girl running into the car had shocked Rollison badly and much of the time since he had been in a state of shock; the pain from the kick hadn't helped at all. Rollison, of course, would blame himself, would find it hard to forgive himself. And Ding Dong Bell—

"God!" exclaimed Grice aloud. "What a mess!"

For Ding Dong Bell, who hated all policemen, would also hate the

Toff – and would blame the Toff for this.

Very slowly, Grice got to his feet, lifted a telephone and ordered a car, then went along to see the Commander C.I.D. and to tell him what was going on. The Commander, young by Grice's standards, sat back in his chair and demanded: "Do you really believe Rollison's got into this simply by c"Yes," said Grice flatly.

"You always did have a soft spot for the Toff," the Commander remarked, half in good humour, half in exasperation. "I'll bet you he's been in it for a long time. Longer than we have, probably. Why don't you send *him* to tell this man Bell?" At Grice's expression, the boyish-looking Commander went on hastily: "Oh, I'm not serious. What's got into you, Bill?"

"I'm worried about this case," Grice replied.

"Then the quicker it's over the better you'll like it," the other said, too glibly. He obviously felt ill at ease, he wasn't usually superficial. "Are you sure it wouldn't be better to send a sergeant or a constable to tell Bell?"

"Not this time," Grice insisted.

Five minutes later he was getting into the waiting car, his detective constable driver holding the door open. As he settled down a call came from behind him, and Detective Sergeant Moriarty came hurrying. "Superintendent! Mr. Grice!" Grice leaned forward as the man drew up. "I'm sorry, sir, but there's a call for you from Mr. Smith at Whitechapel. He says it's urgent."

"I'll take it from the car," Grice said, and leaned across the back of the seat and picked up the radio telephone, flicked it over to the Yard's exchange and ordered: "Put Mr. Smith's call through, please." There were only odd sounds; squeaks, background voices, footfalls. Then Smith came on, and blurted out: "Bill, Ding Dong knows already. He's gone out, breathing fire. Says it's our fault, we must have been chasing her, she was running away. Believe me, that man wants watching!"

"I certainly believe you. Where is he?"

"I don't know."

"How did he find out?" asked Grice.

"Don't know that, either. Bloody fine copper, aren't I?"

"You'll do," Grice said. "I'll send out a general call so that we can find out where he is and what he's up to. Alert your chaps, won't you?"

"They're alerted," Smith assured him gustily. "There's one likely place, you know."

"The hospital?"

"Yes. Or the police station morgue."

"We'll have them both watched," Grice said. "Hold on." He looked up at Moriarty and gave instructions for all he had promised to be put in hand, and the detective sergeant hurried off, proud in his brief authority. "Smithy," Grice went on, "what exactly do you expect Bell to do?"

"Anything from cutting someone's throat to beating him to pulp," stated Smith hoarsely. "If he finds anyone he thinks responsible, he'll murder them. *That's* my opinion, Bill – he'll murder them. He doted on his Daisy."

"If we watch him closely enough he won't be able to do much harm," Grice said.

"To watch him, you've got to find him," Smith retorted.

"Yes," Grice admitted. "Yes." And he put down the receiver.

He drew a hand across his damp forehead, and shivered involuntarily. It was two hours, perhaps nearer three, since he had left Rollison, and a lot could have happened in that time. If Bell had reason to suspect that Rollison had been partly responsible for his daughter's death, anything might happen. He called the West End Division and arranged to have Rollison's flat watched back and front, then settled back again, wondering whether he should telephone the Gresham Terrace flat. Was he making too much of the threat? And was Smith? There was one thing neither of them had taken into account, and that was the human side of the tragedy. If Bell had really doted on his daughter, then he was a man to be pitied and to be helped.

Smith could see only the danger that he might go berserk, of course; and Smith was not an easy man to frighten. On that thought, Grice put in a call to Rollison, and held on; almost at once, Jolly answered in a quiet voice: "This is Mr. Rollison's residence."

"Jolly," Grice said, "the father of the dead girl is a Ding Dong Bell who once served a sentence for robbery with violence, and who's heard of what happened and appears to be on the loose, seeking vengeance. Keep an extra careful watch, won't you?"

"I will indeed, sir. Thank you very much."

"I've put men on guard," Grice went on. "If there should be any trouble, we ought to be able to cope."

"Thank you indeed," Jolly said, and rang off.

Jolly stood looking down at his employer, whom he regarded as his master as in the days of long ago, and also his friend. Grice's voice lingered in his ears, and Grice had been so troubled, even fearful despite his reassuring words, that Jolly had felt impelled to come and make sure Rollison was all right. Absurd, since the flat was empty but for them.

Rollison was breathing evenly, and looked much better; his colour was much nearer normal. He lay back in the easy chair, and had not moved. Jolly turned away from him and, as was his wont when he was emotionally stirred, he paused to study the Trophy Wall. He smiled at the recollection that when Rollison had first hung a hammer there - a blood-stained one used as Exhibit A in a murder trial - he, Jolly, had strongly disapproved. Now there were fifty-four trophies, each in some sense a lethal weapon, and Jolly was curator and caretaker, dusting each exhibit at least once a week and always with great care.

What would the trophy be after this case, he wondered. An income tax demand – or better still, receipt? Anything was possible. Jolly went quietly out of the big room into the bathroom to check that he had cleared it up properly after administering first aid, picked up a piece of the adhesive plaster protective tape, and went into the kitchen. It was now nearly three o'clock, time to start dinner. For tonight, something light and plain, if he judged Rollison's likely appetite aright. He turned to a larder, in a corner of the long, narrow kitchen which overlooked a fire escape and a stone courtyard with a big modern building beyond. He opened the larder door, smiling reminiscently, without the slightest inkling of impending disaster.

A man, inside the larder, shot out both hands and clutched Jolly round the throat. Jolly had no time to shout, to struggle, to defend himself in any way; he had hardly time to breathe and so his lungs were half-empty as those rough, hard fingers bit into his throat, crushing his windpipe, making it impossible to draw breath.

The man was in the shadows of the larder. Jolly could see only his broad face and his bright eyes. And as seconds flew, Jolly knew that the man was going to squeeze and squeeze, until he lost consciousness; perhaps until he died.

Chapter 7

To Die or Not to Die?

Rollison was aware of sounds; and was aware of pressure at his shoulders. He was in the depth of sleep, coming out of it with great reluctance; but coming out. The pressure increased. It was very hard and painful. He felt other pain, in his leg – it was that which first made him alert. He heard the growling voice, then began to distinguish the words.

"Bloody Toff – killing's too good for you. Bloody murdering Toff. I'm not going to kill you in your sleep, don't you worry. I'm going to hang you up by the thumbs and then I'm going to kick you to death."

Now, Rollison was awake; fully awake, because he had the wit not to open his eyes wide; only to listen. The pressure of fingers at his shoulders was like the pressure of steel claws. The muttering went on until suddenly the man snatched one hand away and struck him savagely across the face, roaring: *"Wake up, you killer. Wake up!"*

The man was no longer clutching him but a clenched fist was swinging towards the Toff's face as he opened his eyes. He did two things: moved his head to one side like a boxer, and doubled his right leg and brought it up into the other's groin. The man, thinking his victim barely aroused from sleep, had not dreamed of a counter-attack. There was a curious squelch of sound. The victim drew in a searing breath and began to double up like a knife, hands dropping protectively to his groin. Rollison simply pushed him with outstretched hand and he toppled backwards and then half-fell, half-rolled over to his side. He lay there doubled up, his breath catching as if he could only get air part of the way to his lungs.

Rollison placed his hands on the arms of his chair and slowly levered himself to his feet. When he stood upright he was a little dizzy, but not enough to worry about. His assailant was breathing more deeply but the breath seemed to be drawn, wheezing into his lungs. He would be helpless for minutes, perhaps as long as five. Rollison stepped over him. His left leg was stiff, but not really painful, and he trod lightly as he reached the passage leading to the bedrooms and the domestic quarters.

"Jolly!" he called.

There was no answer.

"Jolly!" Alarm seared through Rollison as he called: and a swift, savage thought – *If you've hurt Jolly* ... He reached the little hall in front of the kitchen and Jolly's other rooms, and then stopped short.

Jolly was on the floor in front of the larder, on his side, knees bent, one arm covering the lower part of his face, unmoving: looking *dead*. Rollison gritted his teeth and the word "No!" was a refrain in his mind. *"No, no, no, no!"* He reached Jolly and bent over him, stretching for the limp arm and limp wrist. "No, no, no, no, it can't be!" He placed his forefinger on the spot where the pulse should be and felt no movement. *"My God!"* he said in a strangled voice, "if he's killed him—" He moved his forefinger a fraction, and felt a stirring. The pulse. He shifted again, pressing a little less. The pulse was slow but quite steady. Jolly wasn't dead, there was no need for that terrible dread. He straightened Jolly out and turned him on his back, pulled a cushion from the kitchen chair and placed it carefully beneath his head.

"I'll be back," he said, as if Jolly could hear him.

He turned away, and went to the study through the lounge-hall.

It was just possible that the assailant had recovered enough to return to the attack, but not at all likely. Standing in the doorway, Rollison saw the man trying to get to his feet. He was grey-haired, hard-looking, and blue about the mouth and green-tinged about the cheeks. He was pulling himself up by the front of Rollison's chair but the going was not easy. He was sideways to the Toff, and he did not look round. His breathing was laboured and did not seem to improve. Rollison waited. The man got to his feet, and Rollison moved so that he was less likely to be seen.

The attacker looked towards the Trophy Wall. It attracted him like a magnet. He reached his feet, supporting himself against the chair, doubled up again as if to squeeze pain away, then straightened up and took a faltering step towards the desk.

He reached it.

He still had to round it before he could reach the wall and the weapons, but obviously that was not what he wanted to do. So, presumably, he had no weapon in his pocket. *Who is he?* wondered Rollison. The man edged towards one corner, leaning all the time against the desk. Still in pain, he grunted with each movement, but there was a single-minded determination to get towards the wall and to take a weapon. Now and again he glanced towards the passage, obviously not dreaming that Rollison was behind him.

He reached and rounded a corner, profile towards the Toff. He had a rugged yet chiselled face, as if hewn out of granite; a rock-made robot. His eyebrows jutted out, and in spite of a broken nose he was handsome; the kind of man many women swooned over.

"Don't you think you've gone far enough?" asked Rollison mildly.

The other spun round on his heels. Surprise and physical effort combined to make him lurch forward, and he grabbed at the desk, touched, lost his hold and staggered away from it. Rollison simply stood staring at him. He swayed and gyrated in the middle of the room, and somehow kept his balance, standing upright but helpless. Full-face, he was less handsome and even more rugged. His eyes were the same violet blue as the girl who had died.

Realisation of who he was shot through Rollison. There was a facial likeness at eyes and eyebrows, at the mouth and chin which betrayed the truth. This man was the dead girl's father.

"You—bloody—murderer," Bell gasped.

Rollison said quietly: "I'm no murderer."

"You murdered my daughter!"

"No," Rollison said. "It wasn't like that at all." He moved slowly towards the other and went on: "But I would have killed you if you'd hurt my man."

"*I'd* kill the pair of you!" cried Bell.

"Yes," Rollison said, quietly. "I believe you would. But it wouldn't get you anywhere if you did."

"At least Daisy would be avenged."

"Vengeance?" Rollison echoed. "Vengeance? Isn't that an empty thing?"

"You don't deny you had something to do with it!"

Very slowly, Rollison replied: "No, I don't deny that. And I shall be haunted by it to my dying day."

"*That* won't be long coming," sneered Bell.

Rollison was startled into a kind of laugh: more, a snort of understanding of the speed of this man's thinking, and his repartee. He sensed a change of mood without being sure what it meant. The other now seemed simply to stare at him, and not to glare with that wild rage; as if something Rollison had said had made him think. Rollison moved still further forward, and motioned to a chair.

"Why not sit down?"

"I bloody well won't."

"Then I will," Rollison said, and dropped into the armchair, leaned back, placed his leg carefully on the pouffe, guiding the movement with his hands, and leaned back. Now, of course, he was vulnerable again. Every time the other moved, he could draw nearer those lethal weapons; this was asking for trouble. But the man stood still.

"You killed her," he stated. "I had it from a newspaperman, he got it from a rookie copper. So I came straight here before the cops arrived. They're in the street now, a hell of a lot of good that is." He drew in his breath again and repeated flatly: "You killed her."

Rollison said: "If I had held her tighter she might not have died."

The other roared : "You admit that?"

"Yes," Rollison answered. "What is the use of trying to evade the truth?"

"Then you did kill her!"

"I don't know who you are," Rollison said. "I don't know whether you have any ideas what she was doing. I can tell you she eavesdropped when I was talking to an Inspector of Taxes, and I wanted to make her tell me why. So I held her. She kicked me and got free and rushed into the road. If you *are* her father" - he raised his hands and dropped them in a helpless gesture - "then I can understand why you'd like to cut my throat. In a way, I'd like to help!" He waited just long enough for the other to open his mouth as if in surprise, and went on: "It was a hell of a thing to happen."

"It was a hell of a thing to do!"

Rollison returned the wild gaze with a cool, resigned one. He leaned further back in the chair, resting his hands in his lap. He did not attempt to turn away as he said: "I didn't have any choice, you know."

"You bloody liar, you didn't have to touch her!"

"What would you have done?" Rollison asked quietly.

"You were having a highly confidential conversation with an official. You discovered that someone was listening-in. It happened to be your daughter but as far as I could know it might have been anyone, even you. Would *you* have just shrugged it off and forgotten it? Or would you have given chase, wanting to know what it was all about?"

The man offered no answer.

He stood only a few feet away from Rollison, apparently recovered from his pain. He looked very powerful, not large but broad and strong-looking. Rock-like, Rollison thought again. He held his clenched fists in front of his chest, as if he wanted to launch himself forward in assault. He was the man who had nearly choked the life out of Jolly, who had intended to beat-up the Toff.

"I'll tell you who really killed her," Rollison said, and he saw the other's lips tighten, his whole body flinch. "Whoever was paying her to spy on me or the income tax man I was with."

"*Tax* man!" breathed the other.

"That's right," said Rollison. "No more, no less. Do you know who employed your daughter?"

The man said harshly: "No."

"Well, she wouldn't spy for herself, would she?"

"Not bloody likely."

"So someone either paid or put her up to it," Rollison said. "And I can tell you one other thing, too." He paused but when the other did not speak, went on in the same quiet voice: "I think she was scared out of her wits by him."

"You fool," the man said, in a helpless voice. "She was scared in case you handed her over to the cops."

"Oh," said Rollison, slowly. "Was she?" He broke off, aware that the other was near breaking point, had passed through an emotional crisis which would take him to the point of collapse. His hands were clenched less tightly now and his body seemed to sag. By now, Rollison had recognised him, and even marvelled that he had not recognised him on sight, although it was a long time since he had seen Ding Dong Bell at Bill Ebbutt's East End pub, the Blue Dog. He had never known him well; he did remember Ebbutt saying one day when Bell had left the pub: "That man can be like a wild dog, Mr. R. I wouldn't ever like to get into a tangle with him." And Ebbutt had told him a little which had gone into one ear and out of the other; but some had stayed behind, including this man's almost pathological hatred of the police. So, danger might spring from what he wanted to say. Without any outward sign, he flexed his muscles and prepared for an onslaught as he said: "What would make an attractive girl like that so scared of the cops?"

The other drew in a hissing breath, his hands tightened, he actually moved one foot forward as he rasped: "She hated the sight of them!"

"Why should she?"

"Because they would never leave her in peace."

"Wouldn't leave *her* in peace?" asked Rollison gently, and after a long time he added: "Or you?" And at that moment he prepared for an attack.

It didn't come.

Instead, the man's lips worked and his body sagged. One hand dropped to his side, with the other he wiped his forehead. He was trembling, too. Rollison got up very slowly and crossed to the William and Mary chest and opened it. Many years ago some vandal had taken out the centre drawers and turned it into a kind of cellaret, with glasses along one side, bottles on the other, including whisky and a syphon of soda water. Rollison took these out, with two glasses, carried them all to the desk, poured a finger of whisky in each glass, and then looked up to Bell, who had not moved.

"How much soda?" he asked.

Bell didn't speak.

"Or would you like it neat?" asked Rollison. He took one glass over so that the man could see it; and he saw as well as sensed the anguish in Bell's mind. He simply waited.

After a while the other man stirred, and focussed his gaze on Rollison, and then on the glass. He took it, almost with a reflex motion, and tossed it down; he did not appear even to gulp. Rollison moved back to the desk and fetched the other glass. This time, Bell took it at once but only sipped a little. And he said: "Ta."

"You need it as much as I do," Rollison said. "You're Ding Dong Bell, aren't you?"

"Yes."

"And Daisy—" Rollison broke off, unable to finish. "Daisy Bell." After a pause he asked: "Was Daisy your only daughter?"

Bell's jaw muscles worked, and he took another sip of the whisky, then said hoarsely : "She was one of twins. The other's Violet. She—" He broke off, finished the whisky at a gulp, and rasped: "Oh hell, bloody bloody hell. She's dead, my Daisy's dead."

And then, as if unbidden and yet beyond control, tears began to flow. He put the glass down, and covered his face with his hands. He moved towards the window, dragging his feet, reached the window but did not take his hands from his face. His shoulders shook but no sound came. Rollison gathered up the glasses and went into the kitchen, where Jolly lay just as he had been left. But as Rollison's fingers touched his forehead his eyes opened with a start, and his body went rigid.

"Take it easy, Jolly," soothed Rollison. "Everything's all right."

"But—but a man—" Jolly croaked.

"He is the dead girl's father," Rollison said. "And I don't think he'll go on the rampage again. Now, let's have a look at your neck."

Both neck and throat were red and swollen and painful, but grew easier as Jolly gargled and Rollison dabbed an alcoholic rub over the bruised skin. Apart from the attempted strangulation, Bell had not injured Jolly, who said with supreme confidence: "I shall have a stiff neck for a few days, sir, but nothing more. I really think we should see what the man is doing, I don't share your confidence, and there are so many weapons on that wall."

"You go in one way, I'll go the other," Rollison conceded.

Jolly took the short way, but he was not in sight when Rollison arrived at the other doorway; undoubtedly he was fascinated as the Toff at the sight before his eyes.

There was Bell, looking as if mesmerised at the Trophy Wall.

He stood on the far side of the desk, one hand in his pocket, studying the weapons, and he appeared to be as interested in the smaller, makeshift ones as in the axes and hammers, daggers and knives, and the ugly piece of iron piping.

There was a velvet glove; a piece of string; some phials of drugs. Each was marked clearly with the names of the people who had killed with these, but in order to read the legends which Jolly had typed about each, one had to be on the nearside of the desk, within hand's reach as well as easy reading distance. But Bell appeared only interested in the actual weapons themselves, not in their history. Could he be selecting one, after all, and still intent on murder?

Chapter 8

Half a Story

Rollison stood at one doorway and Jolly at the other. Without looking away from the trophies, Ding Dong Bell rounded the desk and went close to the wall. Near at hand was a hammer; one used twenty-two years ago as a murder weapon. Bell put his hand towards it and lifted it by the handle, weighing it up and down in his hand. Then, as Rollison's body went tense and prepared for an attack, the man replaced the hammer with a kind of reverence.

At last, Rollison moved forward.

"Quite a collection, isn't it?" he remarked.

Bell started, and looked round; and after a moment he asked: "All yours?"

"All mine and Jolly's."

"*All* Mr. Rollison's," insisted Jolly, stepping from the other passage.

Bell turned his head sharply; stared; and then raised his hands and dropped them by his side. He pursed his lips, and after only a moment's hesitation, asked drily: "So I didn't choke the life out of you."

"Not quite," Jolly replied, tartly.

"And I'm sure that's just as well," Rollison said. "Jolly, what with one thing and another I didn't really get much lunch. What can you fix for us?"

"Certainly some sandwiches and coffee, sir."

"Beer."

"And beer."

"That should do nicely."

"I will see to it right away," Jolly promised, and disappeared.

Now, Bell moved to the desk and leaned against it, much as Rollison had done earlier. He wore a thick tweed jacket over a turtle neck sweater which somehow emphasised his compactness and physical strength. He looked levelly at Rollison, and spoke very quickly.

"So that's the hammer that killed Speaky Mason."

"Yes," Rollison answered.

"I've handled it before," Bell told him. "I was an out of work docker in those days and a plumber's mate on the side. That hammer belonged to the man I worked for, Tim Mayhew. It was stolen from him. You went after him and scared the daylights out of him, Toff, before he admitted it was his. You had a name for it. Don't tell me, I'll remember." Bell did not look away from the Toff but suddenly he began to smile. "Psychological terrorism. That's what you called your method."

The Toff affected to shudder.

"Was I really as corny as that?"

"You'll never know how corny you were! Anyway, Toff, you went after Tim and you got him. That was in the days when a man got hanged for murder." He raised the hammer up and down again as if longing to use it. "I never thought I'd set eyes on it again – or see you in your castle, Toff. That's what they call an Englishman's home, isn't it?"

"Yes," Rollison answered.

Bell turned to look at some of the other trophies again, and slowly shook his head. Without looking at Rollison, who suspected that his eyes were moist again, he began to speak in a low-pitched, grating voice.

"I did a job, twenty years ago. My wife was in the family way and the doctors talked of twins. There was a long dock strike, and I couldn't stay on as a plumber's mate. So I did a job, and got caught. I attacked the man who found me, and he split his skull open on a wall when he fell. Okay – I pushed him hard. I saw red, see – just red. That's my trouble, losing my cool. So the cops came for me. I asked them to let me see my wife, and they wouldn't. Didn't give me a chance, even tried to stop me seeing her when I was on remand. I was sent down for ten years on the day the twins were born."

Rollison raised his hands in a gesture which spoke for itself.

"Didn't see them for eight years," Bell said. "I did my time and got full remission. All I thought about was my wife, Daisy, and the twins – and the coppers. I never did have much time for them, and after that—" He caught his breath and then flung out a question: "You still friendly with bloody Bill Grice?"

Rollison did not hesitate. "Yes."

"So you're still a copper's nark."

"I am still in favour of law and order."

"Law and order," Bell echoed, slowly and bitterly. "If you knew as much as I do about the coppers, you'd vomit. I did know a good one, once. Started a copper and finished as a copper, they never even gave him sergeant's stripes. They don't give you a minute's peace and that's the flicking truth." He flung that out as a challenge, as if calling on the Toff to spring to the defence of the police. Instead, Rollison said: "There are some bad ones and there are some good ones. Have you had much to do with them lately?"

"The further I can keep away from them, the better. But I'll tell you one thing—" Ding Dong paused.

"Then tell me."

"If I can help any poor devil who's in trouble with the police, I'll help him. No two ways about it. There are two sides. I'm on one and you're on the other." The defiance was very sharp in his voice and his expression. "So that puts you and me on opposite sides."

"It looks like it," agreed Rollison, then took a chance, knowingly, anxiously, so apprehensive that his heart actually began to beat faster. "Which side was your daughter on, Bell?"

Everything seemed to drop away from Bell except stark feeling. The grief, held in check until then, sprang naked to his eyes and livid to his face, which drained of colour. His hands and body tightened, yet soon went limp. Rollison moved to sit on the arm of his chair and so ease the pressure on his leg. Bell's breathing began to sound, a faint hiss through his nostrils. They remained like this for a long time. Rollison tried to imagine what was going on in the other's mind; that there was a struggle, bitter and hurtful, was clearly apparent.

Then Jolly came in with a laden tray.

Jolly, of course, had heard the conversation on his transistor, and had judged his entry deliberately to break the tension. He ignored Bell's pose, did not appear even to glance at him, but set the tray on the low table, exactly as it had been set for Grice earlier in the day. The sandwiches had a fresh and appetising look; there was a wedge of cheddar cheese, new bread and a big crock of butter. Without a word Jolly turned, to be back in a few moments with a smaller tray on which were two bottles of a special 4X brand of a beer bottled exclusively for Bill Ebbutt at his pub in the Mile End Road.

He stood back and surveyed the trays.

"I think that is all, sir. Will you have coffee or tea?"

"Tea."

"Very good, sir." Jolly flashed Rollison a glance of understanding and goodwill, and went out. Rollison began to wonder whether he should break the silence; whether the grief which knotted this man's vitals was so great that he could not break through it to speak. Then, Bell moved; stared at the Trophy Wall; went to the window again and stared out. In a croaking voice, he said: "I warned her."

Rollison did not move or speak; in fact he hardly breathed.

"I told her," Bell went on. "I told her it was asking for trouble to work for anyone who was fighting the cops. And she was, she was making too much dough not to be. I told her. But—" He seemed to choke, his hands and shoulders bunched but he went on: "I'd taught her too well, that's the bloody truth of it. Her mother always said I would. I'd taught her to hate the police so much she wouldn't listen to me." Bell's voice faded in a sigh. "That's something I learned a hell of a long time ago. You can't win against them, they always get you."

Rollison let a few moments of silence drift, and then asked: "Who was she working for, Bell?"

"I don't know."

"You do know that if she hadn't worked for him she would be alive, don't you?"

Bell faced him, very squarely, and there was an ugly twist to his lips; a rougher, uglier, note in his voice.

"I know if you had held on to her, she would be."

"Are you sure?" Rollison asked. "I'm a long way from sure now."

"What the hell do you mean?"

"Do you think the man who used her would have let her live long once she was known to be working for him?"

Bell choked: "*Used*. What the *bloody* hell do you mean – *used?*"

"I mean employed."

"You'd better mean employed," Bell rasped. "If you ever accuse my Daisy of living fast and loose—"

"Bell," Rollison interrupted, "it's no use reading things into what I or anybody else says. She was sent to spy either on me or the Inspector of Income Tax. I think more likely on both because he was scared stiff after he had a telephone call while I was with him, and anyone who knew I was interested in him would want to know what I was up to. The moment I'd actually seen her, the man who employed her would know there was a chance that she would be identified and might be persuaded to talk. So he might have arranged for her to be run down. Almost certainly someone did. Who is the man Daisy worked for, Bell?"

"I don't know." Bell repeated, and paused before adding: "And I'm not lying, either. Listen to me, Toff." He strode forward and bent over Rollison, grabbing his coat lapels and lifting him inches from the seat of the chair. He shook him bodily, savagely, teeth clenched, eyes blazing. "You listen to me. You let her go in front of that car. *You* killed her, and don't you think I'll ever forget it."

Very quietly, and without making the slightest attempt to free himself, Rollison said: "Don't you think I shall ever forget it, either. I shall see her running into that car to my dying day."

Bell went still.

Rollison could feel his breath, hot on his forehead. He could see the way the muscles of the other's neck and face worked, how the veins stood out. He saw how the wrinkled lids closed over eyes which had suddenly become shadowed. Gradually, Bell eased himself away, and stood upright, staring over Rollison's head.

Rollison was aware of Jolly at the doorway but Jolly actually drew back. Bell moved now to a chair and dropped into it, and perhaps for the first time, saw the bottles of beer. He stared at them, and at the cheese. Like a man in a trance he picked up a knife and cut off a small wedge of cheese and put it into his mouth. Next he buttered a crust of the bread and put that into his mouth, too. Eating, he levered the top of a bottle, and tipped a glass before pouring out, making a perfect head. He drank deeply, making the froth ring his upper lip. He picked up a paper serviette and dabbed his lips. Then, he spoke.

"Funny how a man can always eat, isn't it?"

"And drink," Rollison observed.

"Drink you can understand, it makes you forget," said Bell shrewdly. "But food – I was in the middle of my dinner when I heard what had happened. I didn't think I'd ever be able to eat again." He paused. "Good bitta cheese, and I haven't tasted bread and butter like this for years. You know how to live, Toff, don't you?"

"Jolly is a good teacher."

"Jolly get this 4X from the Blue Dog?"

"Yes."

"Best beer I ever tasted," Bell remarked. He ate and drank, and Rollison joined him. They did not say a word about Daisy for at least twenty minutes, during which time Jolly brought in tea in a brown earthenware teapot, and with it some kitchen cups. Bell looked up at him. "Tell my wife where you get this butter and cheese from, will you, Mr. Jolly? One of these slap-up places like Fortnum and Mason, I suppose?"

"A small shop in Shepherd Market," Jolly corrected. "I will gladly tell her, sir."

"Mr. Jolly," Bell had said. "Sir," Jolly had remarked, as if it were Bell's natural due. This was not lost on Bell, who smiled faintly, just a curve at the corners of his thin lips. He finished a piece of sandwich, and looked across at Rollison, the smile gone, a hard look in his eyes.

"I don't know who she worked for, Toff."

"But you felt sure it was outside the law."

"Yes."

"Did she tell you so?"

"No. But I knew from the money she spent and company she was keeping."

"Will you tell me who they were?"

"For you to tell the cops?"

"If necessary, yes."

"No," Bell replied, flatly.

"It might be possible to catch the man responsible," Rollison reminded him.

"This job is mine," Bell declared.

"Part of it's mine," Rollison reminded him.

"It's no use, Toff," Bell said. "I won't give anyone away to the cops, directly or indirectly. I can't stop you trying to find out what you can, and I wish you luck. But I don't co-operate with the police."

"Bell," Rollison said, and let the name hang in the air.

"Yes?"

"Do you know whom Daisy worked for?"

"I told you, no," insisted Bell, and the smile hovered again. "The last man who called me a liar got his nose broken."

"I take the point," Rollison said.

"Here's another point," put in Bell, before Rollison could go on. "I won't lie to you, Toff. I may not answer all your flicking questions, but I won't lie."

"I really don't think you will," Rollison said.

"Remember it. There are liars in Mayfair as well as in Whitechapel."

"And fools," Rollison remarked.

"What do you mean by that crack?"

"I mean that you would be a fool to defend criminals against the police. And a bigger fool to take on this task of vengeance yourself. You might get hurt, too. Even killed."

"That would be a great loss, wouldn't it?"

"Your wife and your daughter might think so."

"I'll take the chance."

"Perhaps the time has come when you should stop taking chances for other people," Rollison suggested. "And trying to live for them."

He let the words hang but Bell showed no sense of resentment, not even of understanding, so he went on quietly: "Will you help me find out who employed your daughter?"

"Not if you work with the police."

"I don't have to tell the police everything."

"No, it's no dice," Bell said, decisively. "No, Toff, you and me aren't cut out to work together. I'd wonder what you were up to all the time and I'd wonder if you were passing on everything I told you to the cops. It wouldn't work, I tell you." When Rollison did not comment, Bell went on: "But I'll tell you one thing more, Toff."

"Go on."

"I don't hold her death against you, now. And I won't ever."

"I'm very glad," Rollison said simply. "Very glad indeed."

Twenty minutes later, Bell left the flat and went out into Gresham Terrace.

Rollison stood at the window, watching him, and then was suddenly aware of police officers in the street advancing towards the man. It dawned on him that they would think he had somehow got past them, and would arrest him. Rollison was on the point of flinging the window open when a uniformed policeman appeared from out of his line of vision, and stopped Bell, who simply turned and stared up at Rollison's window, with such derision and scorn on his face that Rollison could see it vividly.

But the Toff spun round, snatched up the telephone and dialled 230 1212, the number of the new New Scotland Yard.

Chapter 9

More of Johnny P. Rains

"What is it, Rolly?" Bill Grice asked.

"Bill, I've just had Ding Dong Bell here, and your chaps have grabbed him down in the street. Will you send out a call to them to go very easy with him? ... He's filled to the brim with hate for the police and is sure he'll never get a square deal."

"I don't quite see—" began Grice.

"Will you fix it first and let me explain later?" pleaded Rollison.

"I'm calling *Information* on another line," Grice promised. "Hold on." A moment later his voice sounded further away but Rollison heard every word. "Flash a message to the car in Gresham Terrace and tell them to handle Ding Dong Bell with velvet gloves. Yes, *now.*" Grice rang off that telephone and his voice became deep in the other. "What's on, Rolly?"

"If we can change his mood Bell might be able to tell us a lot," Rollison said. "In his present mood, he won't."

"Smith out at Division told me he won't listen to—"

"Bill," interrupted Rollison. "Bell hasn't just a wooden chip, he's got a Rock of Gibraltar on his shoulder. He's also grief-stricken. There's much more human being in him than he's shown Smith or any other policeman. Dare I offer a piece of advice?"

"Try me," Grice invited.

"See him yourself. Tell him how sorry you are about his daughter. Tell him all you want from him is any news about the people she worked for. Don't push him: he's like a walking stick of nitroglycerine, likely to blow up at any time. Just let him have a good

66

reason for thinking that policemen can be human beings, too."

After a pause, while Rollison found himself gripping the telephone very tightly, Grice responded: "I can't see any harm in doing that."

"Bless your heart!" exclaimed Rollison with deep feeling, and rang off. He went to the window again, and saw Bell climbing into a police car; this time, the man didn't turn round and look up. The plain clothes man next to the car was scratching his head.

"Wondering what's got into Grice, I suppose," Rollison remarked to Jolly. "Did you hear what I said to Grice?"

"Yes, sir – and echoed every word," Jolly declared.

"Good," Rollison replied, with feeling. "It was the last thing I expected." He raised an eyebrow at Jolly, and went on in a lighter tone of voice: "How's your neck?"

"It really is not too bad," Jolly replied, and added soberly: "I admit that I didn't think I would ever see daylight again, still less feel well-disposed towards Bell."

"I know the feeling exactly," Rollison said. "And now—" He moved so that he would touch the hammer of which Bell had such fond memories, and went on quietly: "I need to think, Jolly. If I need my usual help I'll send for you. If not we'll exchange notes later. Don't be too surprised to have a call from Mr. Slazenger or from private eye Johnny P. Rains. Disturb me for either."

"Very well, sir," Jolly said.

Rollison went to the big armchair, sat back, and stared thoughtfully at the Trophy Wall. The unexpected significance of the hammer soon faded, and although he looked from a silver-handled dagger used by a youth to kill his father to a set of test tubes containing strychnine administered by a chemist to prostitutes so that he could possess them during the awful death spasms, he did not think of the cases, only reflected, and soon drifted on to another. This was his favourite and most successful way of pondering a case in which he was involved. Subconsciously all that had happened went through his mind, and each face, each sentence, each incident, became increasingly vivid. Moreover he could think of what happened to Daisy Bell without being too distressed. It became part of a pattern of events which had started when Watson had been so alarmed by the telephone call, and finished with the death of the girl and the driver of the sports car which had been the instrument of her death.

And the driver's?

That was one of the strangest and most macabre of the things to happen: a young man, dead of an induced heart attack brought on by the impact of car and girl. Yet in this slow and deliberate assessment of what had happened all the other things took on a particular significance: Watson's lined face and Cobb's early near-flippancy and later aggression. The encounter with Johnny P. Rains, and even the brief one with the lame man who had been so exasperated about the lift at Pleydell House.

There had been the autograph-seeking girls.

And there had been the young policeman who had accosted him in Pleydell Street.

At last, everything fell into position, and he stirred. A restlessness always came upon him on such a time as this, and above all else he wanted action. But first, what line should he take? The obvious one was to find out what Johnny P. Rains had discovered about Watson. Rains had been on that trail for – Good Lord! – over six hours. Surely he should have reported by now.

It was nearly half-past five.

Rollison moved again to the telephone, opened the telephone directory and ran down the 'Rs'. He found the number, recognising the digits as being the replacement for the old Grosvenor exchange. He could remember the first three letters of the old exchanges, but the first three digits, never. What use was progress when it created human problems and exasperated or irritated both men and women? He dialled. There was no answer. *Brrr. Brrr.* He dialled again, for there was a reasonable chance that the computerised exchange had computed wrongly. *Brrr. Brrr. Brrr. Brrr.* He rang off, as there was a ring at the front door bell, startling him because he was so preoccupied. He heard Jolly go to the door, and knew that Jolly would check that this visitor was either familiar or proffered no open threat.

Jolly appeared.

"I don't recognise the caller, sir," he said.

"I'll come and look."

Rollison got up and walked through the lounge-hall to the door. Above it was a small object which looked rather like the lens of a camera, in fact it was a form of periscope, which enabled anyone inside to see the person outside.

On this occasion, the man outside was Johnny P. Rains, and as Rollison looked at him he pressed the front door bell again.

"Bring him in," said Rollison. "It's Johnny P."

He went back and waited at the desk, wondering whether this would bring useful information. Soon, there came Jolly's voice, and Johnny's. Oh, confusion! But at least there would be no confusion in their voices for Johnny P's, although pleasant enough, had a very different timbre from Jolly's.

"Please come this way," Jolly invited.

Johnny P. Rains wore the dark grey jacket and the lighter grey trousers which he had worn when Rollison had seen him at Pleydell House. His face was both broad and round, his chin was like a spade with a little point which appeared to have been stuck on afterwards. His fair hair receded at the forehead, giving him a decided widow's peak, and his eyes still reflected that glint of humour. His gaze flickered towards the Trophy Wall but quickly back to the Toff, who shook hands and then pointed to an upright chair opposite his own swivel chair at the desk. Johnny P. was now right opposite the Trophy Wall, and few men could have resisted looking at it. He was not one of the few. Then he turned back to Rollison, and said: "A beautiful golden picture in a beautiful violent frame."

"Or more prosaically, a trophy wall," Rollison said, and waited.

"I've a detailed report," stated Johnny P. "Our Mr. Watson went to three different places, and finally back to his office less than an hour ago." He took a slim book from his pocket and held it towards the Toff, so that it could be read. The writing was small and very easy to read; not copperplate but very nearly as well-formed as type. "He went straight from you to the R.A.C. Club, where he had lunch on his own in the members' dining room. He made a telephone call at one-thirty, left the club at one-forty, walked towards Piccadilly via St. James's Square, and finally called - at two-fifteen - at a house in

Jermyn Street."

"There aren't many houses there," Rollison remarked.

"The bottom floor has been converted into offices, the upper storeys remain a private residence," Johnny P. said. "I chatted with a shopkeeper who lives opposite."

"Was Watson a regular caller?" asked Rollison.

Johnny P. smiled. "I am beginning to understand your reputation. Yes – at least the shopkeeper said he'd been there several times before."

"To the offices or the residence?"

"He couldn't tell," the private investigator replied. "I'm not sure that it matters much, the owner of the import and export business on the ground floor being the owner or tenant upstairs. Quite," Johnny P. added with a grin which in most people would have seemed like a smirk, "a man."

"Man or male?"

Johnny P. laughed. "Male."

"Many girl friends?"

"Nearly a harem."

"You mean, the girl friends live there?"

"Apparently they occupy the top two floors."

"How many?"

"My informant – incidentally, he cost twenty pounds, I hope that wasn't too much – is an observant man but has never been inside the place. He doesn't know how many lovelies live there at the same time, but never less than four, it seems."

"Do they change?" asked Rollison, almost incredulous.

"Frequently," Johnny P. answered. "I think I could get you some photographs but I'd guess they would cost another ten pounds apiece." When Rollison made no comment the other man went on: "Harem or not, there is also a wife. Everything I know is written down, and I'll have some photocopies made of the reports, so that we can each have copies. Shall I go on to the next place?"

"Please," said Rollison, very glad that he had sent this man on Watson's trail.

"He left the house in Jermyn Street at three-fifteen," reported

Johnny P. "He was admitted by a blonde and seen off by the same blonde. He did not look refreshed or relieved, but neither did he look exhausted. What I mean is, nothing suggested that any of the ladies had given him her favours."

"So you don't think it's a high-class brothel?" Rollison asked.

Johnny P. answered with great care: "The shopkeeper doesn't see many men go there. I don't think Watson used it as one, at all events. If anything he looked more harassed when he left than when he arrived. He was obviously afraid he might have been followed, and looked up and down and kept on looking behind him, and eventually he caught a Number 11 bus from the stop near the TWA offices."

"A bus," remarked Rollison, startled.

"To Liverpool Street."

"What did he do there?"

"Bought a ticket," Johnny P. answered.

"To Harwich?" asked Rollison, very softly.

Johnny P. gave a sudden, warm, highly amused chuckle, leaned forward, and said with obvious feeling: "You don't miss much, Mr. Rollison! Half the time you're a jump ahead. Before I have a chance to tell you, you'll be telling me that he booked a ticket to Amsterdam, first-class, with a sleeper on the ferry from Harwich—the *St. George*."

"For tonight?" Rollison asked sharply.

"No. Tomorrow night," Johnny P. told him. "I took a chance on losing him to find out what he'd booked. I'm not unknown at the ticket office there, many an errant husband takes his lady love to the Continent that way. An old friend of mine was on duty, and gave me what information I needed."

"What name did Watson book under?" asked Rollison.

Johnny P. laughed, and said. "Your third point but I suppose that one shouldn't have surprised me. Grey."

"Plain Grey?"

"W. B. Grey."

"Did he have to show his passport?" asked Rollison.

"No," answered the private enquiry agent. "He will have to when he goes on board the ferry, of course, and he'll have to fill in details when he gets to the other side, but he certainly can't show a passport as Watson and go aboard as Grey. So—" He broke off, inviting the Toff to hazard a guess.

"Either the ticket is for someone else," deduced Rollison, "or he has got a passport under an assumed name."

"Which sounds highly improper for an Inspector of Taxes."

"Highly," Rollison agreed. "Well, you didn't lose him afterwards did you?"

"No. He went to the station cafeteria and had some tea, looked through a copy of the *Evening News* and kept a careful watch about him. But eventually he seemed satisfied that he hadn't been followed."

"What kind of disguise did you wear?" enquired Rollison with interest.

Johnny P. Rains laughed outright, then opened the small briefcase and took out a flat, flexible case and a folded lightweight raincoat. In front of Rollison's eyes he took out what looked like a roll of fuzz, and raised it to his face; on the instant, he was a different, elderly-looking man. There was also something un-English about him; he looked more Scandinavian.

"So I am two men," he announced in a slightly foreign accent.

Rollison sat back, smiling, and said: *"Touché."*

"Now there's a remark from a generous man, a man I think I could get along with." Johnny P. leaned back, took off the disguise and folded it and put it away. "To proceed! After he'd taken his time over his coffee, Watson alias Grey took a Number 11 bus back to his office, and when I left, he was still there. That's the lot." After a pause, he went on: "Now that you've had my report may I ask why you wanted it, Mr. Rollison?"

"I'd rather leave explanations until later."

Johnny P. raised his hands. "As you wish."

"What is your fee?" asked Rollison.

"For the day, twenty-five pounds plus out-of-pocket," the enquiry agent replied. "By the week, I come cheaper – twenty a day, including weekends." He leaned forward and although he was smiling there was a hint of anxiety in his expression. He was not as young as Rollison had thought, probably in the early fifties. As far as the indications went he was good at his job; what Rollison needed to find out was whether he was also honest. "Mr. Rollison, you may remember that I asked you if you could spare me a few minutes this morning."

"I remember very well."

"I wanted to ask you to put any leg work you could in my way, I know you by your enormous reputation, of course, and I also know how good Jolly is, but if I may say so, he isn't getting any younger."

"I'm sure he would agree to that," remarked Rollison drily.

"I'm sure, too. You must have a lot in common or you couldn't have got on so well for so long. The truth is there's not much divorce work now that the new laws are getting into their swing, and although I don't much like the bedroom-cum-Peeping Tom work, it does pay a living. I don't mind admitting that I might have to shut up shop, which will be a financial disaster. Men of fifty-two don't find it easy to get work, especially when their only training is in the Peeping Tom business."

Johnny P. Rains stopped. When Rollison did not answer at once, he began to colour. When Rollison still stared at him searchingly, he collected his things together and then began to get up. He zipped the briefcase, and stepped away from his chair.

"Forget it," he said brusquely. "I shouldn't have asked."

"I'm not a bit sure you're right about that," Rollison said, pulling him up short. He could hardly tell this man that a series of mental images had flashed through his mind when he might reasonably have been answering. He had almost said, being sure of the response, that any work Johnny P. Rains did for him would be dangerous, so would he take risks? Then he had the mental flash of Daisy Bell. Next, he wondered whether he had any right to ask another man to take risks, even for money and even though the man himself would almost certainly jump at the chance.

Chapter 10

Legman

"Have you heard what happened in Pleydell Street today?" asked Rollison, as the other looked at him in perplexity.

Frowning, Rains replied: "I heard there was an accident in which a girl was killed."

"Did you hear that the girl had been by the door while I talked to the Inspector of Taxes, and later ran away from me when I questioned her?"

"Good God!" exclaimed Johnny P. Rains. "Is that the truth?"

"The simple truth." In a matter-of-fact voice Rollison told the enquiry agent everything that had happened, still very sensitive to the part he had played in the girl's death, and went on: "There are indications that there could be danger. Acute danger. I don't want you on my conscience as well."

"Oh," Johnny P. said in a rather limp voice. "So that's why you weren't very keen about offering me a job." He pursed his lips. "Well, I see what you mean and I think you may be right." With an empty and rather apologetic smile, he went on: "I don't feel young enough to be a hero."

"I don't blame you," Rollison said, keeping an unreasonable note of disappointment out of his voice. He opened the middle drawer in his desk and took out his cheque book. "Will fifty-five pounds cover your fee and expenses today?"

"*Rather* ," exclaimed Johnny P.

A few minutes later he was speeding on his way. Still aware of the disappointment although he could not reasonably blame the man for his decision, Rollison went to the window, and peered down into the street. No one approached Johnny P. Rains as he walked across the street. There did not seem to be the slightest danger. In fact he had started to turn away, catching sight of the taxi which suddenly accelerated as the private enquiry agent crossed the road.

"My God!" Rollison cried, and tried to fling up the window. But before he had time, before he had actually touched the wooden frame, the taxi had struck Johnny P. Rains and pitched him, a broken body, into the air and on to the pavement.

The taxi put on even more speed and disappeared round the corner which led to Piccadilly.

Rollison did not know what best to do.

He had not told Grice of Johnny P. Rains. It might be proved that the man had come from this house but there was no certainty of that. If Rollison told the police he would have to produce the report, and that would almost certainly mean that the police would investigate the house in Jermyn Street, and by now he was extremely anxious to investigate that himself. But he made himself remember what Grice had said, and he made himself face the fact that this was not simply a hunt for an individual who dealt in crime but with at least one Inspector of Taxes. He had to tell Grice. He went to the desk and touched the telephone; and before he lifted it, the bell rang, making him start.

"Who—" he began, and then recovered himself and said: "This is Richard Rollison."

"This is Ding Dong Bell," Bell responded in his harsh and now familiar voice which held a ring of humour. "I want you to know that your friend Grice isn't like all the other coppers I've known. He's almost human."

"I'm glad you agree with me," Rollison said. "But you didn't ring me up just to say that, did you?"

"No," Bell agreed, laconically. "Can you come and see me tonight, Toff? I might have some news for you."

"Yes," Rollison said promptly. "Where and at what time?"

"25, Quaker Street, Whitechapel," answered Bell. "That's where I live. You needn't get the wind up, Toff. I won't have a reception party."

"You disappoint me," Rollison said, lightly. "What time did you say?"

"I didn't. How about nine-thirty?"

"I'll be there," promised Rollison. "Goodbye."

As he rang off, he pictured Ding Dong Bell's face and tried to recapture the tone of his voice, with its note of rough humour. And two things seemed important, by far the greater Bell's change of feeling towards Grice. Bless old Bill! The other was the use of his own nickname. Ding Dong. Slowly, he realised that the call had driven thought of Johnny P. Rains out of his mind, and another realisation followed: that he, Rollison, had given very little thought to Rains, and had not been deeply affected by his accident. In some way it had been more remote; he had seen what had happened but not so closely.

Yet Rains had been a human being whose life had been cut off; and there must be a possibility - a probability - that he had been run down because of his visit to him; to the Toff. For a few moments Rollison stood quite still, turning that thought over in his mind. Then he lifted the telephone, half-prepared for it to ring; but it did not. He dialled New Scotland Yard, was answered almost instantly, wondered whether Grice would be in and heard the familiar voice almost as soon as he had asked for him.

"Yes? Who is it?"

"*The Toff,*" breathed Rollison, in a puckish moment.

"The—oh!" Grice relaxed, but went on with a grim note in his voice: "Defender of the Wicked, I presume."

"*Is* Ding Dong Bell so wicked?" demanded Rollison.

"If my information is right, and there's no reason why it shouldn't be, he gives a helping hand to any crook who needs it, fresh out of jail or not," Grice said. "His daughters are associates of thieves, and he's spread a 'hate the police' campaign through the East End for years. Venomously." When Rollison didn't answer, Grice went on: "He could be fooling you, Rolly."

"I suppose it's possible," conceded Rollison. "Did you see him yourself?" There was no need for the Yard man to know he had been in touch with Ding Dong. In many ways it would be better if he didn't find out yet.

"Yes."

"What did you make of him?"

"Hard as granite in some ways."

"Ah. And the other ways?"

"I haven't any doubt that he was badly hurt by the death of his daughter," Grice answered quietly, "and I can imagine how sorry you would feel for him; that's what makes me think he could be fooling you. I don't necessarily mean deliberately. I mean the man you saw might be very different from the usual man simply because he's so cut up."

When Grice finished he waited as if knowing that Rollison would need a little time to absorb what he had said; and indeed, Rollison did. He knew Grice as a good human being with the finest of instincts, and also as a man with a penetrating mind. He was not necessarily wrong over this possibility. On the other hand, he did not know the murderous mood in which Bell had arrived.

"Yes, Bill," he said quietly, "I won't overlook that."

"Good!" Grice said more heartily than was his wont. "And don't misunderstand me. There was a quality in the man which I rather liked. However—"

He left that word hanging, and that could only be for a purpose. Rollison, who had been on the point of telling him about Johnny P. Rains, simply waited. The years of friendship with this man had taught him to know when Grice had something of real importance to say. As he waited, he heard the ambulance bell in the street, again; they would be taking Johnny P. Rains away.

Then Grice spoke, and drove away all thoughts of Johnny P., all thought of everything but the morning's hideous affair. It explained – or could explain – a great deal which had seemed inexplicable, but the first impact simply took his breath away.

"The driver of the car which killed Daisy Bell didn't die of a heart attack," Grice said. "That was the first assumption, but the autopsy has shown that he died from an injection of curare, almost certainly injected by a small hollow needle which could have been fired from an air-gun of some kind and possibly by mouth, as by a blow-pipe. We not only have the autopsy report and know that the point of contact was the driver's right cheek, but a small mark is still there, not large enough for a hypodermic needle but quite noticeable under close examination. I'm sending men to examine the car, the actual murder weapon might be in it."

Grice stopped.

Rollison, until then breathing very heavily, said slowly: "So this was murder, Bill."

"I suppose it could have been accidental," Grice temporised.

"Oh, come! Who would send poison darts flying about a public highway by accident?" Rollison rejected the idea and was sure that Grice didn't take it seriously. "Is there anything else?"

"Isn't that enough?"

"Who was the young driver?" Rollison asked.

"We haven't identified him yet," Grice answered. "He had no easy-to-recognise identification or marks."

"Could I have a photograph of him?" asked Rollison.

Grice could of course ask what he wanted with a photograph, and if he did then it might be wise to tell him that he wanted to find out whether Ding Dong Bell recognised the driver. He heard another telephone bell in Grice's office, however, and wasn't surprised when Grice said: "Hold on, Rolly." Then a moment later: "I've got to go and see the Commander. If you really want that photograph I don't see any reason why you shouldn't have one. I'll leave it at the desk. Don't get up to too many tricks, mind. This affair looks like being deadly."

Grice rang off; and Rollison had not told him about Johnny P. Rains; it was almost as if he were meant not to. As he thought this, Jolly appeared, but did not speak at once. Rollison raised his hands and then let them fall, and said: "You got all that?"

"Yes. Be *very* careful, sir."

"I shall be very careful indeed," Rollison said. "Meanwhile, go and get that photograph for me, will you?"

"Shall I wait for half-an-hour, sir?"

"Yes," Rollison said. "That will probably be wise. But I'm going out, Jolly. I want to search the office of Mr. Johnny P. Rains before the police get there."

Jolly looked as if he were going to protest; even, to plead. But instead he said resignedly: "I see, sir. You will go armed, won't you?"

"Yes," Rollison said. "And I'll put on an old suit, too!"

He went into his bedroom and opened the wardrobe. Jolly came in and took a grey herring-bone tweed suit which Rollison had bought off the peg years ago. And he also put out some rubber soled shoes. Rollison, meanwhile, opened the drawer at the bottom of the wardrobe and then pressed a spot on one side. The side of the drawer slid open, revealing a recess in which was a palm gun, some cigarettes which carried tear-gas phials, and a knife with a clip which he fastened just below his left elbow; by flexing his muscles he could work the handle down into his palm. There was also a thick penknife with a variety of stainless steel blades, and a coil of nylon cord. He changed, and put these weapons into his pockets where he could get at them most conveniently – the palm gun, like a thin pocket watch, in his right-hand jacket pocket. On one side was a piece of adhesive cloth which would hold the gun secure against his palm. To fire, he had simply to open a gap between his third and middle finger, bringing the middle finger down on the 'trigger' which was really a catch on the outer edge of the gun.

At close quarters, this gun could kill. Even at twenty feet it could inflict a nasty wound.

"Now I'm all right," Rollison said, as if he weren't quite sure.

"I only hope you don't have cause to use them." Jolly sounded glum and fearful. "What time shall I expect you back, sir?"

"If all goes well at Johnny P's office I shall go straight on to Bell's place, at 25 Quaker Street, Whitechapel, where I'm due at half-past nine. That gives me three hours or more. If I'm not back by eleven o'clock, telephone Quaker Street. If you're not satisfied, alert the police."

"I certainly will," Jolly promised earnestly.

Rollison went out, feeling quite sure that Jolly was at the door, looking up into the periscope; he would stay there until Rollison had turned the first bend in the stairs. Rollison went down slowly, reached the street and saw a crowd still gathered and uniformed policemen taking measurements in the road. There were chalk marks where the body had been. No one took any notice of Rollison, who walked to the end of the street, and saw a vacant cab. Soon he stepped out outside a theatre where there was a line at the box office. He walked along to Pleydell Street.

Everything was as he had left it.

There were the parked cars, with a few gaps, the tall buildings, new and old, the entrance to Pleydell House, dark, perhaps seeming more cavernous. The big lift cage seemed to be coming down. He withdrew in the shadows as it appeared. The secretary who had been eager for his autograph came out, with one of the young men he had seen at the tax office; they were holding hands. Several other people got out, emptying the lift. Rollison stepped in and pressed the top floor button, heard another buzz of sound and as he passed the second floor, saw the elderly man standing there with a sheaf of papers in his hand. He was glaring.

"Can't you stop this bloody thing?"

Rollison felt a twinge of guilt as he went by, but he did not want to be seen closely. He got out at the fifth floor and pressed the second floor bell before closing the gates; with luck, the man would get it as it went down. He stepped to the door of Johnny P. Rains's office, which was opposite that of Bonatti and Firmani, artists in decor. There was a light under that doorway but nothing at Rains's. He first tried the handle; it turned but then stopped. He took out his penknife and opened a skeleton key blade and inserted it in the old-fashioned keyhole. It took only a few moments to turn the lock, and as it clicked, he stood back.

A voice sounded very close to his ear.

"This is your last chance. If you're late in the morning, you'll be through."

A girl said in a gooey voice: "Oh, sweetie pie, what a bad temper you're in. Doesn't he like his little Goosie Girl anymore?" There was a sound, half-laugh, half-giggle, and the door of the artists in decor opened and a blonde came out. She had the longest legs, the shortest mini and the most beautiful flaxen hair Rollison had ever seen; her hair was so long that it looked as if she wore nothing but the mini skirt. She closed the door on the man who was presumably her employer and walked towards the stairs. She did not look round, or she would have seen Rollison. As she started down, she began to hum a pop tune; Rollison suspected that this was for the man's benefit should he open the door.

Rollison opened Johnny P. Rains's door and went inside.

There was plenty of light from the window to show the small outer office; a cover was uneven over the typewriter, that was the only change. The door to Johnny P. Rains's office was closed, but proved to be unlocked.

He pushed it open cautiously.

Whenever he forced entry into house or office, he felt the tension that dropped upon him now. It wasn't exactly fear but was not far from it: a tense apprehension of what he might find. He had run into trouble so often, sometimes into near disaster. He slid one of the tear-gas cigarettes from its packet and put it to his lips, then went inside.

The office was empty; there seemed no danger at all.

He went behind the desk, found the middle, control drawer locked, used a smaller skeleton key and turned and opened the drawer. All the others became unlocked at the same time. He saw photocopies of the report Johnny P. had shown him; and as he opened the drawer wider he saw much more: a thick folder, marked *Kimber, A. L.* and an address in Jermyn Street. There were so many papers and documents here that they could not have been collected that afternoon alone: Johnny P. must have been working on this man for some time.

Rollison opened the folder.

On top was a photograph of a girl, a blonde with hair nothing like as lovely as the blonde's next door. Beneath was another, a third, fourth and fifth.

The bottom photograph was of Daisy Bell.

Chapter 11

Photographs

Rollison touched the photographs and the file very gingerly. He must not leave fingerprints, for the police would come here as soon as they had identified Johnny Rains. He set the pictures aside, and began to go through the papers. There were many notes written in the enquiry agent's neat handwriting, and a story gradually built itself up from the notes, some other, smaller photographs, some newspaper clippings and some pencil sketches. The notes were filed with the latest ones at the front, so the last one was the earliest.

Why does W. go to Kimber & Co.?

Three other notes ran:

Followed W. to K. again... He appears more scared each time ... No sign of monkey business where the floozies are concerned.

Next Rollison came to a report which ran to several pages, also in that neat and very legible handwriting. He read and summarised it as he went along. Johnny P. had become very interested in Watson's movements, particularly his frequent visits to Kimber & Co. in Jermyn Street. The only possible reason, he came to believe, was a tax fiddle of some kind. The report which simply amplified the first notes, showed a picture of Watson becoming more and more frightened. Then there was a note:

If I could find out why it might be very profitable.

Next was a press cutting stuck on to a thick piece of paper. The headline ran:

Tax Man Dies of Heart Attack

Rollison's own heart lurched as he began to read. The cutting was from the *Evening Standard* and concerned an Inspector of Taxes for a North London district. At the foot of the cutting, Rains had written in a bolder hand than usual:

W. very agitated and upset this morning.

Next came some notes.

"I must make contact with someone in W.'s office. He jumps out of his skin if I ask any kind of question ... The blonde girl, Ivy Bartol seems the best bet ... Asked Ivy to have a drink with me today: received a dusty answer! ... Asked Ivy and today she was thirsty ... Nice little girl and attractive above the waist ... Very loyal to W... Confides he's worried and although she didn't say so obviously thinks he's being blackmailed ... Doubt if she will give me much, she's loyal to a fault ... Asked her if she knew Kimber of Kimber and Company and she shut up like a clam, from which I deduce that they do Kimber's assessment at this office ... Is the time coming for a talk with W?"

After this came several more press cuttings, and Rollison read them with growing interest and concern. Two were about Inspectors of Tax who had been involved in accidents; one had died. Another was a cutting in a daily newspaper, headed:

Tax Inspector on Bribe Charge

Rollison, sitting at the desk as if it were at home, heard a sharp click, and raised his head quickly, alarmed. Then he heard another click, and footsteps: the man from next door was presumably shutting up the office and going out. As silence fell again, Rollison turned back to the papers, held by them in a kind of mesmeric intensity.

A note dated the day before yesterday was headed: *Mistake.*

It went on:

"I asked W. why he was so worried today and obviously it was a mistake. He told me to mind my own damned business, and said his work was confidential. *Very* touchy and I doubt whether he will ever confide in me. He went to K. & Co. again today. I must tackle Ivy Bartol tomorrow."

The next note, of yesterday's date was headed:

Why the Toff?

"A turn up for the book today! Ivy tells me that no less a person than the Honourable Richard Rollison, better known as the Toff, is going to see Watson tomorrow. I was careful not to ask many questions. Possibly there is some doubt about the Toff's income declarations. My! What a sensation if it's proved that the great Rollison is defrauding the taxman ... I wonder how much this would be worth to a newspaper if I gave one the tip? I should be able to get a couple of hundred and God knows I need it! ... On second thoughts I might be able to tap the Toff ... He could put some work in my way, especially if I could exert a little pressure ... No, it's no use, I am not a natural blackmailer, I feel a heel even when I think about using pressure ... Still, Rollison might be able to give me some work, it's worth trying."

On another sheet, without a headline, was a note:

"I wonder if the Toff has come to find out what W.'s up to? That would be characteristic of the man, to make dubious returns so as to get into the office and check on W. himself. Highly intriguing! I will try to see the Toff tomorrow and have a word with him."

That was the last note before the report Rollison already had.

Small wonder Johnny P. Rains had been breathing down his neck, of course; and he had seemed so genuinely pleased by their 'chance' meeting. Rollison sat back, flipping over the photographs again, making sure that each one registered clearly on his mind.

He mustn't push his luck: he must go.

There was nothing here he needed to keep from the police, except, perhaps, Daisy Bell's photograph. He studied this again. She was exactly as he remembered, more pretty than beautiful, with fine eyes: violet eyes, he remembered. Violet – like her sister's name. He did not quite know why he wanted to keep this from the police but found himself trying to ease the picture into his inside breast pocket. It was a tight fit, and for a moment he thought he couldn't do it, but it went in at last, only a corner crumbling.

He replaced the files, took off his gloves, and went to the outer office, then to the door. As he opened it he heard the lift cage groaning on its way up. He slipped to the staircase, and was concealed from the lift although he caught a glimpse of three men in it.

One was a policeman in uniform; two were in plain clothes.

He had only time to take a swift glimpse: one man was tall, negroid in features but very white: almost like an albino. The other was shorter and stockier. Rollison was quite sure they were from the Yard or from Division, but had no idea that the tall one was Detective Sergeant Moriarty and the other Detective Officer Odlum. The lift stopped as he hurried down the stairs. Several late workers waited at the lift gates at one floor, and a young couple was going down the staircase.

As he reached the entrance hall, two more uniformed policemen appeared.

He kept to one side, just behind a tall man who would conceal him at least partly from anyone else who looked his way. But neither of the policemen did. He reached the doorway and the spot where he had caught up with Daisy Bell. A police car with a man at the wheel was drawn up and double-parked to his left. He turned right. As he did so he had a swift mind picture of the morning's scene but now there was another factor.

Someone had managed to poison the driver of the car, and that someone must have been standing near here.

No! It might have been someone in a passing car. Someone on the pavement, then, or in a car. Had he seen anything which might give a clue; observed without truly noticing an action by someone near? A man putting a cigarette to his lips, perhaps; or even lighting a pipe. A woman touching up her lips, or even glancing at herself in a mirror; such little things could be noticed but not noted; would be so commonplace as to have no particular significance. But when one made a conscious effort to remember one could see the whole picture again; once photographed on the mind it was never wholly obliterated although it might be covered up for days; weeks; even months. He had to 'see' everything and everyone even on the perimeter of his range of vision.

He 'saw' a man standing nearby, heard his "Oh, my God."

He 'saw' a middle-aged, very distinguished-looking woman, approaching the car briskly, with a well-dressed man. He 'saw' the woman as she passed the driver of the sports car, cutting him off from Rollison's vision for a split second. He 'heard' the man state that the girl was dead.

No one else had been near the driver.

It was possible that someone on the pavement had 'fired' that dart...

No! It was too far, and cars had been in between. He 'saw' something else, too; the far window of the sports car had been closed, only the nearside one had been open. The woman had been close enough to shoot the arrow; in fact she had been close enough to stick a needle into the driver's cheek. Why she should didn't matter at the moment; what he had to do was check his memory closely to make sure that he was right. And he needed to recollect what had happened before. The young driver had stopped. As if in horror he had stared at the girl sprawled over the bonnet. Rollison could 'see' him, sitting strangely erect at the wheel.

Then the woman had passed between Rollison's line of vision and the man.

Rollison's gaze had followed her, had been full of admiration for the person in all that sensation who had kept her head. He must have watched her for a minute – well for half a minute at least. The next time he had looked at the driver he had still been sitting upright.

So – the woman could easily have killed him.

Rollison reached the far end of Pleydell Street and looked across at the closed stalls and shops of Covent Garden. It wouldn't be long before the old market was moved to its new site south of the river; when the faintly sour smell of rotting vegetables and fruit would be gone from here. But that did not matter now.

It was nearly seven o'clock.

He had plenty of time before going to Quaker Street, and there was a great deal he could do, but what *should* he do?

Call Grice?

It was one thing to hold Daisy Bell's photograph; another to hold back such information as he now had about the woman. Yet that could surely wait. There were things he could do for himself much more effectively than the police. He could, for instance, visit Kimber at the house in Jermyn Street. The moment the idea occurred to him it seemed attractive, and the more he thought of it the more attractive it became. If the police went there it could only be to make preliminary enquiries, whereas one whirlwind visit from the Toff might get surprising results.

A sobering thought came: there were at least superficial reasons to believe that Johnny P. Rains had been run down because of what he had been doing, and because he had been to see him, the Toff.

Rollison crossed the road to a telephone kiosk and called Jolly; but there was no answer. He put down the receiver and studied the entries in the telephone directory. There were two:

Kimber, Adrian & Co. Exp/Imp., 76 Jermyn Street, W.1
Kimber, Adrian V. 76 Jermyn Street, W.1.

Rollison moved away from the kiosk and walked to Mount Street, past a famed restaurant and an equally famed antique shop. He turned towards Berkeley Square, where traffic was comparatively light. He began to walk briskly across the heart of London which was so much part of his life that he could never pass any monument, such as Roosevelt's in Grosvenor Square, without feeling at least a reflected pride. He strode at rare speed, passing the big clubs and the commercial buildings, and then towards Piccadilly Circus. Not consciously thinking, he reached the corner of Jermyn Street and felt more sure than ever that he should visit Adrian V. Kimber. He slipped into the foyer of a world-famous restaurant where he was well known, and called his own number; Jolly was still out, probably getting the photograph Grice had promised. He went to the *maître d'hôtel* who was at his little desk, a kind of guarded entrance to the big room which sparkled with bright silver and snow-white damask against a background of dark red. The man, short, heavy, with beetling brows, did not recognise him at first; then his eyes lit up.

"It is Mr. Rollison!"

"Hallo, Jean-Pierre," Rollison said. "Will you do something for me?"

"But of course! Anything!"

"Telephone my flat in half-an-hour and tell my man Jolly that I shall be at Mr. Kimber's house in Jermyn Street, if I am wanted for the next two hours."

He expected no more than an over-effusive "But certainly, Mr. Rollison." He expected the expressive face to go through changing emotions, making this a major performance. In fact he wasn't really thinking of the *maître d'hôtel* as much as what he would do when he reached Number 76, Jermyn Street.

Slowly, however, he became aware of Jean-Pierre's change from eagerness to shadowed concern. It would have been remarkable in any man but was doubly remarkable in this one. For obviously Jean-

Pierre was startled and after a moment it was evident that he was even a little shocked. He opened his mouth as if to comment, gulped, and then spread his arms and bowed slightly from the waist.

"If M'sieu Rollison wishes."

Rollison looked at him keenly, and then said in an easy voice: "What is it, Jean-Pierre?"

"I am very glad to perform a service for you, m'sieu."

"But you don't approve of my visiting Mr. Kimber?"

"Please. It is none of my business, Mr. Rollison," Jean-Pierre insisted, but obviously he was unhappy about the task. "I will telephone Mr. Jolly as you request."

There were only the waiters, busy in the big dining-room and two couples at a small bar in a corner, as well as the doorman, close by the door and peering into the street in case someone came up, on foot or in a taxi. None of these people could see, still less hear, Rollison as he held a hand towards the *maître d'hôtel* and asked more seriously than before: "Tell me what the trouble is, Jean-Pierre. Please."

"I regret, m'sieu, it is not your concern and I should not have allowed you to see how I reacted. *Please.* I will telephone—"

"I know I might be going into danger," Rollison said.

"I've never met this Mr. Kimber and I'm not sure I shall want to meet him again, but meet him once I must. What can you tell me about him, Jean-Pierre?"

The man's dark eyes began to glow, the hint of disapproval and of self-reproach began to fade. He drew closer to the Toff, his manner now conspiratorial and not in any way aloof; he even rested a finger on the back of the Toff's hand.

"M'sieu," he said. "Mr. Kimber does not pay his bill."

"Good Lord!" exclaimed Rollison, taken completely by surprise. He could at once understand Jean-Pierre's reaction and disapproval while marvelling that a man who appeared to have a lot of money and certainly lived expensively should offend such a restaurant as this. Driven to desperation, Jean-Pierre and those who ran the establishment with him could telephone every high-class restaurant in London and warn them against giving Adrian V. Kimber cre"That is unforgivable," declared Rollison at last. "I shall be very careful of Mr. Kimber."

"One thing I will say," went on Jean-Pierre. "He has a fine taste in beautiful young women!"

He sped Rollison on his way, and Rollison, assured that Jolly would know where he was, walked briskly along to 76, Jermyn Street. It was a narrow house with fresh white and black paint and highly polished windows: surely the home of a wealthy man. The nameplate was of good quality, the doorstep glistened. Rollison rang the doorbell, not yet sure what he intended to say or do; this was a job he could play by ear, which was really his favourite method.

He heard sounds inside the house, drew back a little, speculating on whether the blonde would open the door. Then the door was opened, and it was all he could do to keep his smile set.

For this was the woman who had approached the sports car in Pleydell Street and could have killed the young driver.

Chapter 12

Adrian V. Kimber

The woman looked at Rollison without speaking, as if puzzled. He said: "Good evening," and waited as she responded, but he knew that she was looking at him more intently every second.

"Can I help you?" she asked.

"Is Mr. Kimber in?" enquired Rollison.

After a pause, she said: "Yes, but I'm not sure whether he's free."

"I wonder if you would find out," Rollison asked, and turned on his most charming smile.

"I am sure he would want to know who has called."

"Oh, yes," Rollison was apologetic. "Rollison – Richard Rollison."

She had recognised him, he felt sure; and her start of surprise was pretended. But she smiled in turn and stood aside for him to pass. The moment he was inside these offices he had a sense of luxury if not opulence, of glistening chandeliers and old mirrors and at least one fine painting opposite a large Italian carved mirror. There was a flight of stairs with paintings on the wall, and another chandelier at the landing.

"Would you prefer to go by lift?" she asked.

"Is there one?"

"It's very small."

"Then may I walk up?"

"Of course," she said.

He stood aside for her to go ahead, but she hung back, saying pleasantly: "Please go up." So he led the way and she followed. She was very close on his heels; in fact she seemed to be breathing down his neck, which was absurd, she must be at least two treads behind him. As he drew nearer the landing he heard piano music - Debussy, so light and delicate - and for some reason, quite unexpected here. He remembered the driver of the sports car, and what Grice had told him.

One sharp stab of pain – and death.

He reached the landing. The woman might not be guilty, of course, but she had been so close to the driver, and it seemed too much of a coincidence that she should be in Adrian V. Kimber's house.

She stepped by his side.

"Will you come into the living room," she asked. "My husband hates to be disturbed while he is playing; but I'm sure he won't be long."

"I will gladly wait," Rollison said.

The piano sounded so muted and gentle; beautiful; far removed from violent death. Rollison had a sense that the player was lingering over each note, lovingly. The notes came with such purity as they passed a door which stood ajar, and entered a room which overlooked Jermyn Street. This was long and narrow, with a soft light glowing from concealed lamps. There was a corner couch; some low tables which he thought were Japanese, one vase in a glass cabinet which at first glance might be Ming. The carpet was of many but subdued colours; the paintings on the walls were Japanese or Chinese, with at least one large papier-mâché panel from Saigon.

"So you are Mrs. Kimber," Rollison remarked.

"Yes, Mr. Rollison." At close quarters she was very pleasant-looking, with a good and fair complexion, neatly groomed grey hair; a gentle-looking woman of much elegance. "What will you have to drink?"

"A Tio Pepe, perhaps," he suggested. "If you have —"

"Of course," she said, and went to a corner cabinet of intricately-carved black wood with many inlays of what looked like porcelain pictures; he knew this was hand-carved and hand-painted and suspected that it came from Bangkok. She opened it to reveal glasses and bottles; it reminded him vividly of the William and Mary cabinet in his own room. She took out a bottle of Tio Pepe and poured out, handed a glass to him and said: "Do sit down."

"Thank you." He chose a spindly but comfortable armchair as Mrs. Kimber took her own glass and lifted it to him.

"Your good health."

"Cheers," Rollison said.

He was beginning to adjust, although still nonplussed. Looking at this calm and attractive woman it was virtually absurd to think of her as a murderess. He knew better than to jump to conclusions and yet first impressions always mattered very much.

"May I know what you want to see my husband about?" asked Mrs. Kimber.

"Wouldn't it be better to wait until you can both hear?" he asked. "It's very pleasant here, and I haven't had the easiest day."

"As you wish," she agreed, and sat on the couch.

The sound of music continued with haunting gentleness. The room was so lovely and the lighting so soft that the world outside seemed to be shut out; there was no sound of traffic, no intrusion although they were in the heart of the West End. Mrs. Kimber's eyes glowed. A pearl necklace at her throat glowed, too. The round neck of the black dress showed enough of her skin to set the pearls off to perfection. The hideous things of the day seemed to fade and he was in a dangerous mood of contentment. He thought: *contentment*. He wondered with a strange contraction of his muscles whether there was a drug in the Tio Pepe but decided that there wasn't: that his mood was due to the contrast with what had gone before.

The music faded.

He was aware of it and of the coming meeting, but he did not stir. There was a footfall, outside the room. Mrs. Kimber got up, keeping the glass steady in her hand, and moved towards the door. She could see the landing more easily than Rollison. He saw her smile as she said: "Darling, we have a visitor." She waited until Kimber was in the room, and added: "You would never believe: it is Mr. Rollison."

Kimber was tall and fair-haired, younger than Rollison had expected. He did not pause as she spoke but glanced at Rollison. He had an abrasive kind of handsomeness which showed despite the soft lights. Abrasive? There was a great contrast between the looks of the man and the music he had been playing.

"Well, well" he exclaimed. "The Toff."

"Isn't it a surprise?" asked the woman, with laughter in her voice.

"The surprise of the week, at last," agreed Kimber. "Good evening, Mr. Rollison. What made you so bold as to walk into my parlour?" He looked down at Rollison, close to him, crowding him deliberately. Rollison could not resist a feeling that despite all the indications to the contrary, Kimber had known he was here and was fully prepared. His wife moved to the cabinet but Kimber hid her from Rollison so that he could not tell what she poured out. "You have a reputation for loquacity," the man went on. "What has struck you dumb?"

The woman laughed; softly. The man looked round and took a glass from her. "Thank you, Lila," he said, and put the glass to his lips. "To your death," he said mockingly, and drank deeply.

Rollison said lightly: "To all the life you deserve to have."

"I'll drink to that." Kimber withdrew a foot or two, and went on in his rude and arrogant manner: "Now that you're here, aren't you going to ask me a lot of questions? The impression I have been given of the handsome, elegant Toff is that he hurls a torrent of penetrating questions at his victims, breaking down their resistance by the very brilliance of his cross-examinations. But a moment, please. Lila, is he handsome and elegant enough?"

"Oh, undoubtedly," Lila Kimber declared.

"So you meet one qualification," Kimber went on. "Now match it with that penetrating wit and daring, and we shall know that your reputation does not lie."

All this time, Rollison had been watching and listening with fascinated interest. It was hard to believe it was really happening, harder to see why – unless this man thought it possible to break his nerve and believed compulsively in the advantages of attack. Now, he sat upright, placed his glass on a small table, gripped the arms of his chair and stood up. Kimber, too close, had to move back a pace. He frowned, as if he disliked Rollison taking any kind of initiative.

"What about those questions you've come to ask?" he said sharply.

"But I haven't come to ask any questions," Rollison retorted lightly. "Why should I, when I know the answers? Do you mind if I smoke?" He drew a small packet of cigarettes from the pocket where he had kept the palm gun which was now firmly stuck to his palm.

"Then what the devil *have* you come for?"

Rollison lit a cigarette, blew smoke to one side, and then answered: "The kill."

"*What* kill?"

"The kill in the case of the terrified taxman.

"You must be mad!"

"Don't be silly," Rollison said with a touch of impatience. "Your wife or an accomplice killed the driver of the sports car this morning. I suspect Daisy Bell rushed into the street because she was very frightened of failing you. I am reasonably sure you arranged to have Johnny P. Rains killed this evening because he had discovered too much about you. I'm as sure that you knew he had come to see me earlier. You will guess that he talked freely, and you will fear that I know as much as he did – which makes me even more dangerous to you than he was, as I know how to use my knowledge better. Now!" His voice had a decisive note. "I came into your parlour, Mr. Kimber, because I am quite sure I can walk out again whenever I wish."

All this time, Kimber was staring as if unbelieving.

Lila Kimber had been out of the room, but she was back, standing just behind her husband, looking as if she, too, could not believe her ears.

Rollison was not sure what to expect next; not even sure of the situation. He felt better standing up than when sitting down, and he moved towards the door, although by no means sure that even if he started to go out, he would be allowed to. He did not think for a moment that he was alone in this apartment with the Kimbers. The palm gun gave him comfort, but he had a sense that he was the victim of a strange practical joke. He watched Kimber closely, tensely.

Suddenly, the man threw back his head and roared with laughter.

And Lila Kimber laughed on a low-pitched, happy note.

And other women laughed—

Not women, Rollison saw; not really women, but girls.

Four or five of them streamed into the room and brought new brightness and gaiety. They were dressed as modishly as fashion models, one with mini-skirt, two with midis, one in an ankle-length dress which, apart from two swathes half-covering her breasts, seemed to start from the waist. They moved about with curious flowing motions, all looking at Rollison, bright-eyed and eager.

"It *is* the Toff!" one girl cooed.

"Isn't he handsome!" breathed another.

"And so elegant!" sighed a third.

The one in the long-skirted, near-topless dress slid her arm through his, and her hand slid down his arm, fingers perilously close to the palm gun. She squeezed, and looked round and up at him.

"You're lovely, Toff. But you couldn't have meant what you said, could you?"

Another girl, the top of whose red head came only as high as his shoulder, peered up at him; she had amber-coloured eyes; cat's eyes.

"But you did mean it, didn't you, Toff darling?"

"Oh, he meant it," declared Adrian Kimber. "He always means what he says – don't you, Mr. Rollison?"

"But he couldn't think you're a *murderer*, Adrian dear!"

Rollison hooked the palm gun into position with his thumb, then put an arm round each girl and squeezed them very tight. Both were looking up at him and clinging; lips parted. He kissed the redhead and kissed the near-topless, and one of the others called: "My turn!"

"Isn't he darling!"

"Isn't he precious!"

"But such a bad guesser," declared Kimber. "And this time so hopelessly wrong."

"Johnny P. Rains fooled you," a girl declared.

"Johnny was always a great one for fooling."

"I wish I could say he always would be," said the Toff in a carrying voice, and for a moment they seemed shamed into silence. Kimber's laughter faded, most of the girls looked shocked, but that lasted for a moment, and the redhead put her hands upon him, shamelessly again, and put her pert, pretty face up towards him, the cat's eyes glowing.

"Take me to bed, Toff," she pleaded. "I've a lovely one upstairs."

"Don't be mean!" cried Topless. "Take me!"

"Me!" another cried.

"Why not *me*?" a fourth pleaded.

Suddenly, they surrounded him, five young beauties in all, holding his hands, his arms, his waist, clinging, clutching. Beyond them Kimber, an arm about his wife's waist, was smiling with great satisfaction. It could not have been more obvious that this had all been planned; it must have been arranged very quickly when Kimber's wife had gone out of the room. Whatever the truth of that, here he was, surrounded. Even if he tried it would be difficult to shake them off. He felt a rare kind of breathlessness, and his heart began to beat very fast when one of them pressed his cheeks in with her forefingers and kissed him on the lips, while another slipped her hand into his trouser pocket and began to jingle his loose change.

Kimber called out: "See the great Toff."

"Isn't he *darling*," Lila Kimber called.

"Why don't you help yourselves to a souvenir?" Kimber suggested.

"His tie!" a girl cried.

"His shirt!" cried a second.

"His pants!" shrilled a third.

And they meant it.

Mrs. Kimber had most certainly put them up to this game and Kimber would see that they carried it out. Rollison did not wholly understand except that Kimber wanted to shame him, to mock his masculinity, to make him feel a fool. Two girls were already pulling at his jacket, and once the sleeves came off the knife would be revealed; and once they had his jacket, most of his weapons would be gone. Understanding stabbed through him. That was probably the basic idea: to disarm him.

But his cigarettes with the tear gas were in his hip pocket.

"Hold it!" Kimber cried, and Rollison saw him on a chair with a movie camera in his hand, focussing it. "Now take his pants!" he cried, and two of the girls pulled Rollison's jacket off and another began to unfasten his belt buckle. "Won't you be proud of this picture, Toff?" called Kimber. And then Rollison saw his wife with a still camera focussed on him. "What a headline!" Kimber went on. "Orgy for the Toff!"

"The Toff's sex-life," suggested the redhead.

"The Toff in his harem," said Topless.

They appeared to be enjoying the game thoroughly, delighted with what they were doing. Even Kimber seemed genuinely happy, his wife gay and free and younger as she clicked away; and the camera whirred. They seemed now to take it for granted that Rollison knew that he was beaten and could do nothing to help himself. One curious thing was that the girls were so soft and pretty that he did not want to hurt them, although soon he probably must.

He thrust his left hand into his pocket as if to hold up his pants, and there were shrieks of laughter. Two girls snatched at his wrists to pull his hands out. He gripped the cigarette case, then let them pull his hand, and dropped the case to the floor. One of them reeled backwards from the effort, and gave the Toff the chance he needed, for momentarily he had both arms free. He simply swept them round so that two girls went staggering away, and there were now only two in front of him. He swung his arms forward now and gripped their wrists and twisted. Each gasped in unexpected pain, and each went staggering.

Rollison bent down and picked up the cigarette case, as Kimber cried: "That's enough!" As Rollison turned to look at him, he went on savagely: "Now they'll really tear you apart! You'll wish you'd never been born."

Rollison simply opened the cigarette case and tossed it to the floor. The 'cigarettes' spread out, the tear gas billowed, suddenly the girls began to gasp and cry out, and Kimber was swearing on a high-pitched, venomous note.

He levelled an automatic at the Toff, who jumped quickly to one side.

Chapter 13

Vanishing Trick

Rollison heard the crack of a shot, but felt nothing.

He saw the gun waver in Kimber's hand, then saw Lila, hands at her eyes, lurch against him. The other girls were reeling helplessly, tears streaming from their eyes, and the straps had slipped off Topless and she was wholly topless now. Rollison picked up his jacket, hoisted his pants and rushed towards the door, the tear gas biting at him although he had not once drawn breath since hurling the case.

He breathed at the door where the air was clear.

He went out, grabbed the handle, took the key and slammed the door. He turned the key in the lock and slipped it into his pocket, then hurried to the stairs. The girls were crying out and screaming, Kimber was yelling: "Open the windows!" The noise reached a high crescendo; if a window was opened alarm would be raised in the street outside.

Rollison fastened his belt and slipped on his jacket.

He was gasping for breath and his eyes were stinging, tears beginning to roll down his cheeks. The problem was to make the right decision and he hadn't had much time to think. It would be useless to call the police, the only charge could be against him, each of the others would give evidence. Yet he wanted time to search this house, from the offices below to the attic. As he opened a window in a small room on the right these things were crowding through his mind. There was a baby grand piano in one corner and electric candles on each side of the music rest.

He could go downstairs and into the street and escape—

But this might be his only chance of searching the house.

He turned back to the landing. There was less noise now, and no sense of an alarm being raised. Kimber was saying something but Rollison could not hear the words. If he pressed closer to the door he would lose what precious minutes he had. It was possible, just possible, that Kimber would call the police himself – but if he had any sense he would keep them far away from the house.

Then what he, Rollison, needed was a reason for bringing the police here.

He moved away from the door of the locked room, and hurried through the rest of this floor. There were two bedrooms each with a bathroom leading off, a large kitchen and a small dining room; that was all. He ran up the stairs to the next floor, where surely the girls were housed.

Who were they? What did they do?

The landing had a dim light but seemed full of shadows. One seemed to move. He kept close to the side of the stairs, palmed the gun, and crept up. The shadow faded, it was a trick of the light. He reached the landing, aware of the odour of scent and powder, but puzzled. Did *six* girls live up here? What was the place? He half-laughed at the thought of a harem with Kimber's wife as the harem mistress. Bizarre notion! The layout here was much as on the floor below, and he found a living room and a smaller kitchen. The other rooms were spare bedrooms, not simply empty but obviously for the time being unoccupied. They were too meticulously tidy to have been used by any of the girls now in the big room.

Then where had the girls come from?

Upstairs? There was certainly an attic floor.

Did they come from their own apartments, each day?

Could there even be a connecting passage with a house next door?

Rollison thought: I ought to get out of here.

At the same time, he thought: I'll never have another chance to search.

He found the narrow staircase leading to the attic. There was a smell of dust; emptiness, and in any case there certainly wasn't room for the six girls. He reached the landing. Straight ahead was a bathroom and on either side a bedroom; it was a pleasant little flat but dusty and unlived in.

So the girls must come from next door.

How could he get there?

He had not seen anything to suggest a doorway which couldn't be easily explained, but there were blank walls which could conceal sliding doors. It shouldn't take long to find out.

He felt under sharp pressure of time. It could not be long before Kimber and the others broke out of that room, and once they came at him he would have no chance at all. He could remember only too vividly how the five had set on him, and there was no doubt that they *could* have torn him to pieces.

He ought to get away from here.

Instead, he crept down the stairs to the first floor landing, listening intently. Last time he had heard the subdued voices; this, he heard nothing. That puzzled and troubled him. He moved closer to the locked door. This wasn't imagination, and there were no muted sounds: only silence.

What had happened?

Could—could they have been too susceptible to the tear gas?

"Oh, nonsense!" he exclaimed aloud.

But his heart was thumping. The silence seemed absolute and oppressive, there was no sound from above or below.

He recalled the way the girls had suddenly appeared, as if out of nowhere. Obviously they could burst out of this silence with the same suddenness.

He had to find out what had happened to the seven people in that lovely room.

He listened more intently at the door and at the keyhole, as Daisy Bell must have done at Watson's office door. If anything, the silence seemed more profound. The key was still in the lock. He turned it gingerly, half-expecting a great surge about him once the door opened, but there was still no sound. The lock clicked. His heart leapt. Silence followed. He waited a few seconds and pushed the door open gently. The light from the concealed lamps still glowed. A flashing neon light from the street spread a red glow – on, off, on, off, satanic, sinister. He pushed the door open wider.

No one was in sight; there was no movement.

He stepped inside and peered behind the door, but that part of the room was as empty as the rest.

The smell of tear gas had almost faded, and the windows were closed again.

The scent of perfume lingered in one corner, and the faint odour of cigar smoke; that was the only indication that anyone had been here in the past hour or so. He stepped further into the room, then thought he heard a sound behind him, and spun round. No one was there. He took the key from the outside of the lock and locked himself in; at least he could not be attacked from the landing without warning.

But from the room?

His glass, on the table by the frail Chippendale chair, was still there, with a little of the Tio Pepe left. The glasses which the Kimbers had used were gone. He moved about, discovering that ashtrays had been cleaned and the room tidied up. Chairs had been put back into their place. No handbag, no camera, nothing to remind him of what had happened remained – except his own glass. It was as if Kimber had whispered *abracadabra* and the whole place had emptied, and made to look as if everything that had happened in here had been in Rollison's imagination.

He studied the room.

The common wall between here and the house next door had two Japanese paintings and the papier-mâché plaque, but no light fittings. He moved closer towards it. The surface, covered with a dull-finished, off-white paper, looked unbroken but at two places the joining line showed where different rolls of wallpaper had been used, showing more clearly than usual. There was a fractional gap in the corner; he was as nearly certain as he could be that this was the position of a sliding door. There was no need to look further for the explanation of the vanishing trick.

There would probably be another such secret entrance upstairs to the flat next door.

He stood looking at the corner, trying to see how the door was controlled; there seemed no blemish except a knot in the dark-polished wainscoting. He went down on one knee and examined the wood, and shone a pencil torch on the darker spot. The knot, at first apparently a natural blemish, was too clearly artificial; and there was a hair-sized circular gap surrounding it. He had little doubt that this was the control button but he did not want to test it yet.

He had wanted to search this house, but now that would probably be a waste of time; they wouldn't desert it if there were anything worth finding.

From the moment he had been here, there had been anti-climax, but none so great as this. He simply did not know what best to do. He *could* send for the police. He could—

He moved swiftly back to the music room and the photographs and studied each one closely; without surprise he saw an excellent portrait of Daisy Bell in a feathery costume, as of a chorus girl in a musical. Of the other photographs he recognised Topless but not the redhead or the others. For the first time he had a reason for calling the police; they would come like a shot when they knew Daisy Bell had been here. He stretched out for the telephone on a wall bracket near the piano, actually touched the shiny black surface, and then nearly jumped out of his skin, for the voice of a man seemed to come from his side; Kimber's voice.

"You don't think I'd leave the telephone connected, do you, Rollison?"

Rollison spun round. No one was in sight, but Kimber uttered a droll kind of laugh; and the laughter seemed to be echoed by a woman; perhaps by several women. The sound came from above his head, but he could see no grating; and he could not imagine how Kimber knew he was at the telephone.

"Scared?" Kimber asked, sneering. "You haven't even begun to be scared yet." He barked a laugh. "Ever been hoist with your own petard before, Toff? ... Remember your early days when you used to use what you called psychological terrorism against the East Enders? I remember. What's it like to be on the receiving end of psychological terrorism, Toff? Or should I call you what the yellow press dubbed you – Crusader against Crime?"

Rollison's thoughts flashed back.

Ding Dong Bell had used that same phrase when he had lifted the hammer from the Trophy Wall. Bell was old enough to remember those early days in the Toff's 'crusade against crime' but surely Kimber wasn't. Or had the light and the colour of his hair and complexion been deceptive in the soft light; was he more grey than fair? Was he nearer fifty or fifty-five than the forty he had looked? Rollison has no way of telling but whatever his age Kimber was well-briefed in the days when Rollison had first begun to work in the East End, where crime had then been concentrated.

He *had* used psychological terrorism; he *had* worked by scaring the wits out of the men he worked against; it *had* succeeded time after time. And it was now being used against him. Kimber was trying to scare the wits out of him; he had from the moment he had stepped into the big room, when he had unleashed the girls on him.

"Lost your tongue?" mocked Kimber. "That's not the first thing you're going to lose, Crusader. Before I let you go out of here there won't be much of you left."

Subdued laughter sounded in the background, as if all the girls had heard Kimber and were highly amused by what they believed would soon happen to him, the Toff. The voice sounded very near, the mocking, confident note was unmistakable. And if it meant anything it was that he, Rollison, could not get out of here by his own free will.

Why not?

How could Kimber stop him?

He felt his heart thumping again and at once realised that this was exactly the effect Kimber wanted: to unnerve him, to make him fearful. The almost unbelievable thing was that he, Rollison, had come here by chance. Kimber could not possibly have expected him, unless he had taken it for granted that after his visit to Johnny P. Rains the next place would be here.

What was there to stop him from getting up and walking out of here?

One thing was certain: he had to try.

The laughter had faded and Kimber was silent, no doubt that was part of his tactics. Rollison moved slowly and sat on the piano stool, expecting an interruption at any moment. None came. He must school himself to show no reaction if Kimber did speak or more laughter came. He hitched the stool up and spanned the piano keys, remembering the piece from Debussy. He was not a classicist but had played a great deal in his earlier years, and now began to play a tune with strong overtones of the days of the Second World War, a period of some of his most active days in the East End – the *Warsaw Concerto*. As he played, the piece seemed to call out some quality in him. From playing lightly, little more than strumming, he began to play with heart and fervour. Now and again he missed a key but it did not affect him, he played on and on until the last triumphant bars.

The sound of music echoed and re-echoed, fading very slowly.

No other sound followed; it was as if by playing the tune he had hurled defiance and the others had been repulsed at least for the time being. Was that nonsense? He only knew that his nerve was quite steady and he had no sense of apprehension as he got up and went back into the big room. He made sure he had missed nothing, and there was nowhere here to search. There might be downstairs, but he doubted it.

Then he glanced out of the window.

Across the road, parked in a driveway to a small building which stood back from the road, was a police car. Standing about nearby were men whom he felt sure were plain clothes policemen. And, marvel of marvels, Jolly was looking across at the house! Rollison threw up a window, leaned out, and called: "Jolly!" He saw his man and all the others start and look up. He had never seen such a smile of delight on Jolly's face, and on the instant Jolly stepped into the road.

A car was coming from the Haymarket.

Rollison's heart turned a somersault as he bellowed: "Careful!" The brakes of the car screeched, Jolly backed in alarm and the car missed him by inches. A policeman threw up his arms. The driver, while the car still moved, shouted: *"Want to get yourself killed?"* and then drove on. Jolly, obviously abashed, looked right before he came forward again. Then he crossed the road while Rollison hurried down the stairs. The door was not locked, and he opened it as Jolly and several policemen came in.

"Just wait until Mr. Grice arrives," a detective sergeant said to Rollison, obviously in disapproval. He was the tall, pale-faced man, who introduced himself as Moriarty.

"Do you know why the police are here?" Rollison asked Jolly.

"Yes, sir. Mr. Jean-Pierre telephoned me and I called them after I failed to get a reply to a telephone call to this house."

"How long ago?" asked Rollison.

"Only half-an-hour or so, sir, about nine o'clock. Jean-Pierre appears to have hesitated for some time whether he should telephone and tell me what he knew – which was simply that Kimber ran up a very substantial account, and did not pay. When there was no reply I telephoned Mr. Grice and arranged to meet the police here."

"We have no search warrant—" Moriarty began.

"I was attacked and might have been seriously hurt—" began Rollison.

"That's good enough for *me,*" declared Moriarty.

Twenty minutes later, every room in this house had been searched; and the room next door had been entered through a sliding panel operated by the 'knot'. Everyone of Kimber's party had gone. The two upper floors of the adjoining house had obviously been occupied by women, there were oddments of make-up, and odds and ends, but all the wardrobes were empty. So were the downstairs rooms, actually offices like those at Number 76. Later there would be a longer and more thorough search, but Rollison felt that the vanishing trick was complete and that Kimber had known well in advance that trouble was on the way for him here.

When the main search was over and nothing had been found, a car pulled up outside and Grice stepped out.

Moriarty, a shadowy kind of individual, seemed to fade into the background completely.

"Hallo, Bill," Rollison said, as Grice entered the hall. "What made your chaps listen to Jolly?"

"We discovered that the driver of the car which ran into Daisy Bell at one time worked for the man Kimber," Grice replied. "We searched the driver's flat, a small one in Chelsea, and found some instructions from Kimber. There was sufficient to justify coming in a hurry when Jolly called. Our chaps knew Kimber and his wife had left just before we arrived, and were waiting for them to come back before questioning them. Instead, you turned up. Now I'll have your explanation, please."

Grice, obviously, was as disapproving as Moriarty, who stood nearby.

Chapter 14

Hand-in-Glove

Rollison could tell the whole truth, and bow to the wrath of the police for going to Johnny P. Rains's office; or he could tell part of the truth, and say that he had no particular reason to suspect Kimber, but had played a hunch. Grice would probably believe that, and would not complain so bitterly.

Rollison told the simple truth as briefly as he could. Moriarty, so curiously negroid in appearance, emerged from his self-induced shadows, and glared even stronger disapproval. When the story was told, Grice said grimly: "You really did want to get your throat cut, didn't you?"

"Oh, I don't know, Bill. It was only a social call, when all's said and done."

"Social call my hat! It was your old trick of getting to a suspect a few hours ahead of us and trying to scare the wits out of him." Grice was not so disapproving as he sounded, his manner was quite relaxed. "You shouldn't have gone to either place without telling me. One of these days, please God, you'll have the sense not to do things on your own. I would like a written report of what you found at Rains's place and what happened here."

"You shall have it," promised Rollison, humbly.

"Tomorrow morning," Grice insisted.

"Tomorrow morning," agreed Rollison. "May I go now?"

He sounded so meek that Grice actually laughed, but Moriarty simply removed his disapproval further into the background. Jolly, a distant observer of what had been happening, moved forward, opened the street door, and stood aside for Rollison to pass, saying: "The smaller car is outside, sir." No one in the street seemed particularly interested in what was going on at Kimber's. The small car, an Austin 100, was parked only twenty yards away, and Jolly asked: "Will you drive?"

"No. You," decided Rollison.

Soon, Jolly was threading his way through traffic in St. James's Street and then in Piccadilly. No one followed and no one took any notice of them. Neither of them talked. There was a parking place at one end of Gresham Terrace and Jolly slid the little car in, having only inches to spare. A big car passed, very quickly, and for the first time Jolly spoke.

"That was very careless of me in Jermyn Street, sir."

"Yes," Rollison agreed. "But I'm not sure whether you were as careless as I was."

"In going there?" They were walking side by side towards Number 25.

"Yes," replied Rollison. "Do you have any idea why Grice was so forbearing?"

"None, unless it was that he realised that Detective Sergeant Moriarty was too disapproving, sir."

They reached the door of Number 25, and as Jolly opened it with his key, Rollison looked up and down as well as across the street. No one appeared to be watching, but there was no way of being certain they were not being observed. Jolly opened the door cautiously, and then allowed it to bang heavily against the wall, his way of making sure that no one was hiding behind it. Rollison needed no telling that Jolly was as much on the alert as he, and so as conscious of potential danger.

They walked up the stairs, Jolly behind Rollison. At each landing they paused to look both up and down. No one followed, no one was waiting to 'receive' them, and the front doors of the other flats, one at each landing, were closed. Even when they reached the top floor and the Toff's flat they were extremely cautious. The tiny periscope worked in reverse, and Rollison peered into this. As always, Jolly had left a light on in the lounge-hall so that they could see whether anyone lurked in there.

No one did.

Yet Jolly opened the door quietly and very carefully, while Rollison went in, half-prepared for attack. None came.

Jolly went along the domestic passage and Rollison through the study-cum-living room, opening every door. They met at the doorway of the spare bedroom.

"Everything appears normal, sir," Jolly remarked.

"It does here, too," Rollison replied, and he felt truly relaxed for the first time since Adrian Kimber had entered the big room at the Jermyn Street house. He went into the bathroom, washed, slipped out of his heavy suit, placed all the weapons on the bed, and put on a pair of grey slacks, slippers, and a lightweight smoking jacket. When he returned to the big room, Jolly had set the dining table in the alcove, and was standing by the hot-plate, where a casserole dish streamed.

"I put this on earlier, sir, in the hope that you would be home. You have had far too many snacks recently."

"I'll bet you have, too. Lay a place for yourself, Jolly. I'll tell you what happened as we have dinner."

"Thank you indeed," Jolly said, as if it had not occurred to him that Rollison might suggest this.

The casserole was of oxtail, with haricot beans and small dumplings, perfectly cooked and appetising; there were also boiled potatoes. Rollison helped himself to the succulent mess, and Jolly took rather less. They were halfway through, and Rollison was already through with the visit to Johnny P. Rains's office, when there was a loud ring and a sharp *rat-tat* at the front door. Rollison jumped; Jolly placed his hands on the table as if to get up. There were no other sounds as Rollison got up slowly, went to the lounge-hall, and looked up at the periscope mirror.

The landing and upper staircase were empty.

Rollison opened the door a crack and made sure no one was hugging the door, then looked down at a packet placed close to the foot of the door. It was wrapped in brown paper, and was about the size of a small tin of biscuits.

"Be very careful, sir," Jolly urged.

"I will. Make sure there's no one at the back, Jolly."

"Very well, sir."

"If this thing ticks, I won't bring it into the apartment," Rollison promised.

Reluctantly Jolly went to the back door, which led from the kitchen, to make sure that no one was trying to force entry there, relying on the call at the front door as a distraction. No one was. Rollison, meanwhile, crouched over the brown paper packet, but heard nothing. He picked it up, gingerly, and placed it close to his ear. Then he carried it into the big room, placed it on the desk, and began to tear the Sellotape off. Jolly appeared, and said urgently: "That is exactly what Mr. Grice was doing when *he* was nearly killed, sir."

"I remember," Rollison said. "But I don't think this is lethal – at least not in the explosive way." The tape came off and he pushed the wrapping paper back carefully, fully aware that Jolly had very good cause for fear.

Swiftly, his immediate alarm faded for this was a tape-recorder, with two spools secured to it, also by Sellotape. There was no sound at all. Rollison took off the securing tape, then opened the recorder; a small cable was tucked inside, and attached to it a bayonet type plug.

"You know what this is, don't you?" Rollison asked heavily.

"A recording of what happened at Jermyn Street, sir?" hazarded Jolly.

"I think so," Rollison said.

Jolly plugged in a table lamp and took out the bulb. Rollison, having examined the recorder and seen how it worked, plugged into the lamp socket, and then placed a spool, marked in pencil '1' on to the spindle and attached one end to the other spindle. He switched on, and immediately the spool began to turn and a humming sound followed, until it was broken by Lila Kimber's voice, saying: "Darling, we have a visitor." After a pause she went on in a lilting voice: "You would never believe: it is Mr. Rollison."

Faint background noises followed. Rollison could remember the tall, fair-haired Kimber, so much younger-looking than he had expected.

"Well, well!" he exclaimed from the tape. "The Toff."

"Isn't it a surprise?" asked Lila Kimber, laughter in her voice.

It was more than laughter: it was laughter at the Toff. That was much more apparent now than when Rollison had actually heard her. The recording emphasised the note of mockery in both voices, and the edge of cruelty, too. Rollison turned up the volume and motioned to the table, and they went back, Jolly taking their half-filled plates away and using fresh ones for more steaming hot casseroled oxtail from the hot plate. They both sat facing the tape-recorder and taking in every word.

Kimber's voice, so often harsh and savage, such as when he drank: "To your death." His, Rollison's, response: "To all the life you deserve to have." After a while, the duelling stopped, and there was a curious intensity in Rollison's accusations which piled up on one another until they sounded utterly damning. And Kimber did not deny a single charge. Even Rollison, who knew so well, held his breath to wait for the man's reaction, and was taken by surprise by the roar of laughter.

A moment or two later Lila and the girls were laughing.

Rollison could 'see' what had happened but in a way the scene must have been as vivid to Jolly, for odd words and phrases, some of which Rollison had not caught, came clearly. Each of the voices came over well, the girls all sounded as if they were thoroughly enjoying themselves; and there was an impression that all of this had been mutual.

"It *is* the Toff," a girl cooed.

"Isn't he handsome," breathed another.

"And so elegant," sighed a third.

Laughter, mockery, the sound of voices from different places so that it was easy to believe that they surrounded him. The sudden: "Take me to bed, Toff. I've a lovely one upstairs."

Then Topless: "Don't be mean! Take me."

Rollison finished what he was eating. Jolly got up without a sound, to get fruit, salad and whipped cream from the sideboard;

and a cheeseboard containing those varieties which he knew the Toff most liked. They ate and listened to the ribaldry, to sounds of the girls tearing into him, and of Kimber saying: *"Now take his pants! ... What a headline! Orgy for the Toff!"*

"The Toff's sex life."

"The Toff in his harem."

There were a dozen other phrases, and a note more of gaiety than malice, as if they were all really enjoying what they were doing. And Kimber and his wife kept on laughing in the background and urging the girls on. The most conspicuous thing to Rollison, however, and he was sure it would be to others, was his own silence.

He did not say a word; until quite suddenly and breathlessly the girls began to gasp and cry out with pain. Kimber roared: "That's enough! ... Now they'll really tear you apart! You'll wish you'd never been born."

There was gasping; crying; squealing; and, blasting above all other sound, the roar of a shot.

The sounds which followed were anti-climactic: the closing of the door, Kimber shouting "Open the windows!" and then suddenly silence, as the recorder was switched off. The utter silence was as compelling as the recording at its wildest, and Jolly and the Toff sat without speaking, until at last Jolly said: "A very disturbing experience, sir."

"I won't pretend I enjoyed it much," admitted Rollison.

"It is quite remarkable that you escaped from the room, at all."

"Don't ever let me be persuaded that my little gadgets like tear-gas cigarettes and a palm gun are melodramatic," Rollison said feelingly. "They really work." He finished the cream and juice at the bottom of his dish, then cut himself a small piece of Gouda. "As a reasonably dispassionate listener, Jolly, what do you make of all this?"

Jolly stood with a cheeseboard in one hand and a cheese knife in the other. For the first time since the recorder had begun to play back Rollison studied Jolly's face without being deeply preoccupied with his own thoughts. His man's lips had a rim of white and his eyes were glassy.

"I am not dispassionate at all, sir. I am extremely angry."

"I'm beginning to see that you are," Rollison replied, half-smiling. "Try not to be."

"But I am, sir. To think such a thing could happen to a man whose *only* concern is the good of others is sickening. Quite sickening. *And* unjust."

"We don't live in a just world," Rollison murmured, "and I have more of its goods than most."

There was defiance in Jolly's eyes, in spite of his philosophical attitude, and for a moment it looked as if he were going to vent some of his anger on the Toff. He made a palpable effort to retain his self-control, breathed very deeply, and inclined his head.

"I shall get the coffee, sir," he stated firmly, and turned towards the kitchen.

A smile hovered on Rollison's lips as he watched his man, but it slowly faded. He knew how Jolly felt, and knew also that Jolly was always most vulnerable to ridicule. He could accept the facts of danger, of routine, of scoffing from the Press sometimes and of disapproval and rebuke from the police. None of these things had more than a fleeting effect. But if anyone attempted to make a fool of the Toff, that went very deep indeed.

The telephone bell rang.

Rollison got up immediately, and stepped down from the dining access to the telephone on the big desk. As he picked up the receiver he heard Jolly announce formally. "This is the residence of the Honourable Richard Rollison."

Immediately the response came: "And is the Honourable Richard Rollison in his residence?"

It was Kimber. A sharp intake of Jolly's breath told Rollison that the note of mockery in the voice had betrayed his identity, and this would be a great test of Jolly's power of recovery. The pause which followed was a long one; Jolly was fighting for his self-control. At last he replied quietly enough to show how he had won this struggle.

"I will find out, sir. Who is speaking, please?"

"One Mr. Adrian Victor Kimber," answered Kimber in a tone suggesting he meant to burst every vestige of Jolly's self-control.

"One moment, sir." Jolly put the receiver on the table and a moment later appeared in the big room, where Rollison was now sitting on a corner of the table, holding the mouthpiece against the palm of his hand. "What do you wish to do, sir?" he asked.

"I'd better find out what he wants," Rollison said. "Go back and tell him so, will you?" He put the receiver to his ear and waited until Jolly told Kimber: "Mr. Rollison will be on the line in a moment, sir," then spoke in a casual voice: "Yes, Mr. Kimber?"

Kimber was startled enough by the matter-of-factness to ask: "*Is that Rollison?*"

"Yes. Or if you prefer it, the Crusading Toff. What can I do for you?"

"Surely—surely you've heard that tape!"

"I've just finished listening to it," Rollison said. "It's a very accurate rendition."

"Don't you know what it *means?*"

"I think I know what you think it means," Rollison said briskly. "That it makes me look all kinds of a fool and so holds me up to ridicule that you can use as blackmail. But you can't. Offer it to any television or radio company, do whatever you like with it and whenever you like. It won't worry me, Mr. Kimber. And I don't think it will worry the police, except to check the things I accused you of. Where are you speaking from?"

"I'm at—" began Kimber, then broke off and caught his breath. He muttered what sounded like: "You cunning swine," and then banged down the receiver. Rollison put his down more slowly, and he heard Jolly's go, too. He sat swinging his leg until Jolly came in, also smiling and in a very much better mood.

"My congratulations, sir," he murmured.

"Thank you, Jolly. What did you make of him?"

"There is little doubt that he thought you would not want the tape heard by anyone else, sir, and that he expected to use it so as to exert influence over you. He now knows that it won't serve that purpose." Jolly paused, frowned again, and went on: "Presumably you will have to let Mr. Grice hear it."

"Yes," agreed Rollison. 'Yes indeed. But unless he turns up again tonight, I think I'll sleep on it. I imagine the police have more than enough to do, and I could do with—"

He broke off, in sudden and fierce alarm, and shot an almost despairing glance at the electric star-shaped clock set in the wall on one side of the fireplace. He slid off the desk at the same time, and went on in a helpless-sounding voice: "It's half-past ten. I'm an hour late for Ding Dong Bell already, Jolly. Find out if he's on the telephone and tell him I'm on my way, will you?" He hurried out to his room to change back into the clothes he had worn at Kimber's, angry with himself for having forgotten. There were all kinds of reasons and excuses but none made him forgive himself for such an oversight. He set great store on the outcome of the relationship with Bell, and he should never have allowed anything to get in the way.

When he reached the big room again, Jolly was putting down the receiver.

"I'm afraid there is no answer, sir."

"With luck, he's gone to the Blue Dog," said the Toff. "Call Bill Ebbutt and tell him I'm coming and ask him to stand by and pick up the pieces."

Chapter 15

The Blue Dog

In the later days of the Industrial Revolution, when industry, and trade were expanding as fast as the British Empire, a vast extension of London docks had been followed by the building of tens of thousands of tiny houses, little more than hovels stuck together in long terraces. Each front door opened on to the street. Each house had a tiny 'garden' now usually a path of concrete or hard gravel, at the back. Most were served by alleys at the back with wooden doors leading into each yard. Dotted about this great mass of tiny buildings, each of which often housed six, eight, sometimes even ten human beings, were public houses and churches. The pubs had mostly been put up to catch the trade as more and more people moved to London's East End, the churches had come afterwards. One of the originals had been the Salvation Army Citadel.

Not far from the Whitechapel Citadel was the Blue Dog. This lay behind the Whitechapel Road, near the docks. Now over a hundred years old, it was as resplendent in blue and white paint today as it had ever been. The inn sign, of a blue dog sitting and looking up at an invisible master, was London-famous.

So was its owner – Bill Ebbutt.

Unlike most of the nearby public houses, the Blue Dog was a 'free' house, which meant simply that it was not tied to any particular brewery but could stock whatever beers it chose. One small East End brewery manufactured 4X, 3X and 2X for the exclusive use of the Blue Dog. The 4X was a kind of Thameside Guinness, considered by many to be a great source of strength, a tonic in time of anaemia, a lift at times of work-fatigue and – it was often whispered – even possessing aphrodisiac qualities. Possibly that was why it was most in demand on Friday and Saturday nights.

There were four main bars: the public, the saloon, the cocktail – a new addition – and the 'private'. The biggest of these was the public bar, where there was standing room only on a thickly sawdusted floor. The atmosphere here was still dark, mostly from the blue smoke of limp-looking hand-rolled cigarettes made from pungent-smelling shag. These were still called coffin nails. To meet both the demand and increasing laziness of many people, Bill Ebbutt had big stocks of these wrapped in rolls often held together by a limp rubber band. These were rolled by old cronies of the landlord, in the Gymnasium. This home of many a boxing hope was built round the corner from the Blue Dog, and greatly patronised by old fight fans, old pros, and many a young hopeful. Ebbutt paid for this work in beer and, when necessary, a snack from the public bar, for contrary to the general concept of the Welfare State many people in the East End of London could be hungry too much of the time. Ebbutt also helped to run youth clubs, clubs for old people, work-at-home projects and other businesses largely financed by Richard Rollison.

With the mass of London docks on one side, with waterways and docks and locks and basins spreading half-a-mile or more from the river's edge, and with one of London's main arteries to the East on the other, this particular part of London was like a wedge, starting where the Whitechapel and Commercial Roads forked. Huge warehouses, cinemas and shops, lined the main streets. While much of the area, including forbidding Wapping High Street, was exactly as it had been for a hundred years, the warehouses, rising like huge prisons with walls at least as thick, were much newer. Huge patches of the terraced hovels had been blasted out of existence by Nazi bombers, still more had gone the way of slum clearance and huge new estates of bigger and better houses, high-rise and low-rise apartment blocks, had sliced through the terraces.

Few of these were near the Blue Dog. In fact the pub and the Gymnasium were on a kind of island, the tallest buildings for a long way around, the centre of a web of old original Industrial Revolution hovels. All these roads led to the Blue Dog.

In two of the small terraced houses, with a communicating door in between, lived William 'Ding Dong' Bell. In one, both of his daughters had been born and reared. And past these houses, known as 25, Quaker Street, drove the Toff about eleven o'clock that evening. At one corner was an old chapel, or Friends' Meeting House, long since deserted by the Quakers who had moved to larger meeting houses not far away. One section of this old chapel was now used by a printer who set his own type and treadled his single flat-bed machine and did a thriving business in wedding cards, dance tickets, even tickets for 'A Night of Fair Fights' at Ebbutt's gym, every Thursday of the year.

Rollison, for a reason he himself did not fully understand, had come in his Bentley. It was perhaps a gesture of defiance, intended to prove beyond all doubt that Kimber had not weakened his nerve. The car was a pale blue Continental, not new but obviously well-beloved. It glistened beneath the streetlamps, which were still of gently hissing gas. The door of Number 25 was closed, but he pulled up outside it. He knew that at every other front window, both on street level and the first floor, there were faces; and that many a *rat-tat-tat* on common walls had alerted neighbours to go and see, and many a small child was despatched through the gates or over the garden walls to alert neighbours.

It was the East End's form of the tom-tom; a grapevine which had been growing for a hundred years. In the beginning it had simply meant *'The cops!'* but of recent years it had come to mean many things, by no means least *'The Toff!'* So hundreds watched as he got out of the Bentley and approached Number 25, and hundreds heard him knock.

There was no answer.

He tried again but no one came; Ding Dong and his Daisy were out, probably at the Blue Dog. What had happened to Violet, Rollison wondered, on the night of the day that her sister had died? He saw a dozen small boys in the shadows, and the bolder householders opened their front doors. No one spoke. Rollison got into the car and closed the door – and something clanged against the body; a stone hurled from nearby. Another struck a wing, yet another the glass of the rear panel, but he shot the car forward and was soon out of range.

He didn't like what had happened. Apart from the damage to the car, there was possibility that the stone-throwers had been bribed. Who else but Kimber would have arranged it? He turned two corners and parked outside Ebbutt's Gymnasium. Lights showed at windows and doors, a few elderly men sat on wooden benches, and most stood up when the Bentley arrived.

Men called out: "Good to see you, Mr. R.!"

"'Ow's the Toff tonight?"

"Wotcher, me old Charley!"

"Keep an eye on the carriage for me," Rollison pleaded as he climbed out; and there was a chorus of promises, while more men came from the Gymnasium itself, calling out greetings. They would watch the car and deal short shrift to any youngsters who threatened damage.

He walked to the corner and then to the Blue Dog, at the next.

It was not dark, but poorly lit. Two or three of the gas mantles had burned themselves out and the small floodlight which usually illuminated the Blue Dog sign was out. And round here it was chilly, with an east wind. Up and down the road were parked cars, mostly small; a few lights glowed at the front windows, but mostly it was gloomy and quiet – until Rollison pushed open the door of the public bar. There was in fact a small light and sound trap but as the inner door opened there was a babble of voices, an assault on Rollison's ears, and bright fluorescent lighting assaulted his eyes. There were perhaps forty people here, mostly men, and each seemed able to talk and drink at the same time.

Three barmen were busy at the old-fashioned wooden handles, which looked like truncheons standing on end. One of them glanced up, saw Rollison and jerked his head towards the left, to a doorway which led from the public to the saloon bar. The nod presumably meant that Bill Ebbutt was there, and, observed by a few but accosted by none, he went through.

Ebbutt, massively pear-shaped, was behind the bar.

Ding Dong Bell, Mrs. Daisy beside him, was at a table in a corner. There were a dozen or so people in the room but Rollison was aware only of Ebbutt, briefly, and of the Bells. He called: "Hallo, Bill," and heard Ebbutt's wheezy: "Evening, Mr. R.," and then crossed to the Bells.

"I'm sorry I'm late," he said. "I was held up."

"I like a man of his word," Bell said, without getting up. "Anyway what I wanted to tell you won't do any good, now. The damage is done, Toff. You made a bloody fool of yourself."

He stopped.

And a moment later, into an uncomfortable silence, came the sound of Kimber's voice, on the tape: and it forced everyone to silence as it went on and on. The door to the public bar opened, and men appeared, to listen; where there had been a babble of noise there was silence except for the voices on the tape.

They were threatening voices.

Tempting voices.

Mocking voices.

Seductive voices.

Five different voices, each distinct from the others.

When it reached the spot where the girls had called to him to take them to bed, there was a guffaw of laughter from the public bar, followed by another, more raucous. Across it and across the voices on the tape came Ding Dong Bell's voice: "Keep your mouths shut! I want to hear the rest again, if you don't."

Silence fell. Everyone was staring at the Toff and listening intently. Ding Dong Bell was smiling faintly. Ebbutt was looking ill at ease. Someone out of sight sniggered: "Even the Toff couldn't take five, one after another."

"That's not the point," another man called. "Could they take him, Charley?"

Now, barkeepers were moving about the room, looking under tables, trying to find out where the recorder was. Two peered underneath Bell's table, two others behind the curtains, then one of them discovered it. No larger than a box of matches it was stuck to the side of a quart bottle of 4X. He stretched out his hand for the bottle, which was within arm's reach of Ding Dong Bell, who was staring at the Toff.

"Don't touch it," Rollison called. "Don't spoil their fun, Dave."

'Dave' was the barman near the tape-recorder; a wizened man. He drew back and glared round at Ebbutt for instructions. Ebbutt shrugged his big shoulders, and Dave moved back to the bar and the voices went on and on, the laughter and the mockery.

Suddenly, Rollison realised that the part in which he had so roundly accused Kimber had been cut from this tape. So had other parts which could have shown him in good light. Someone laughed, and another sneered: "A lot of bloody good the Toff is, these days." And suddenly, as the tape died away, a man threw a bottle across the room and it missed Rollison's head by inches and smashed against the wall.

"That's enough!" roared Ebbutt.

But the atmosphere here was suddenly dangerous. More bottles flew, one of them close to Ebbutt. When he ducked it smashed bottles of whisky and gin and other spirits on the shelves behind him. The door from the other side, the dockers' bar, suddenly opened and more bottles were hurled – and a knife flashed within six inches of the Toff's face.

Bell grabbed his wife's arm and rasped: "Come on!" and he dragged her towards the door.

Rollison called: "I'm sorry, Bill."

He took out the cigarette case and tossed cigarettes about just as he had at Kimber's house. Suddenly the rooms were filled with coughing, gasping men and women; and the first to suffer, for he was asthmatic, was Bill Ebbutt. He disappeared, coughing helplessly. Rollison fended off one bottle and then another but for the moment the danger was over, the men were helpless as they wiped their eyes and staggered about.

The Toff moved towards the door to the street; and as he reached it, all the lights went out in the Blue Dog.

At least six people were trying to get into the street when Rollison reached the door. Fresh air was sharp against his nostrils and his lips, but he was better off than any of the others and moved quickly towards the nearest corner, then to the other side of the street. He stood there dabbing at his eyes and watching as the patrons of the Blue Dog came streaming out of the two main doors, most of them coughing, one or two retching as if violently ill. A car slowed down as people ran blindly into the street. Another car roared up, and suddenly Rollison was touched with panic. *Kimber killed with cars!* Headlights blazed, shining on dozens of people, men and women, on a dog held on a leash. Brakes screeched. A car veered towards Rollison, and the only chance he had was to climb up over a doorway, a shallow porch of which jutted out. He stretched up and hauled himself on to the porch. The car slewed round, passed the doorway by inches, and sped towards the corner.

Rollison dropped down to the ground again.

A man, nearby, came at him with a broken bottle levelled at his face. He thrust out a foot and sent the man reeling back, but another came at him from the other direction and he had no doubt that they meant to kill. The best he could do was to fight back with the doorway behind him so that at least he need not fear an attack from the rear.

Men whose faces were covered by stocking masks came at him, one from the right, one from the left. He could not hope to deal with both; he had a strange feeling of calm with an acceptance of the fact that he was fighting his last fight. A knife flashed; a bottle smashed on the wall close to his head and sprayed him with jagged pieces. He saw a third man rushing at him, had only a split second in which to decide who to tackle first.

Suddenly men came rushing from the Blue Dog and from two corners, yelling, brandishing Indian clubs and ropes; and whistles sounded, very like police whistles. The attackers turned and ran, the rescuers, from Ebbutt's Gymnasium, drew close to the Toff and flung a protective cordon about him. Already he knew that not one of them was under sixty.

Next Ebbutt came, at the double, gasping and wheezing. The whooping and the yelling stopped, Ebbutt drew level with the Toff and said with deep anxiety: "My Gawd! Look at your face!" Then he turned to one of the other men and went on urgently: "Get Lil. Tell

her the Toff's face is cut about something awful." Then he took
Rollison's arm and led him across the road as blood oozed from a
dozen cuts caused by the pieces of broken glass.

Chapter i6

Ding Dong

'Lil' was Bill Ebbutt's wife.

She was now a Major in the Salvation Army, since rules and regulations had been relaxed so that, having married outside the Army, she should not be banned. She had trained in first aid as a girl, during the war, and she cleaned the cuts quickly and efficiently, here and there dabbing on a lotion which stung enough to make Rollison jump. But soon the pain eased, and Lil stood back from the chair in her living room and surveyed her patient with obvious satisfaction. Behind her, grampus-like, Bill Ebbutt held a towel and a bottle of the lotion.

"You'll do, Mr. R.," Lil said. She was small and thin-featured and sharp-eyed, wearing an expression which always seemed bad-tempered; but in fact she was one of the most even-tempered of women, most of her fervour coming when she was clanging on cymbals in the Salvation Army Silver Band. "How does it feel?" she added as an afterthought.

"Not bad at all," Rollison admitted, with relief.

"You *look* almost back to normal," Ebbutt declared. "Never seen so much blood, Mr. R., proper put the wind up me you did."

"Just surface cuts," Lil maintained. "Lucky thing none of them splinters caught you in the eyes, Mr. R."

"I couldn't agree more," Rollison said fervently.

"Now you sit there and I'll get you a cup of tea," Lil said, and she turned and added severely to her husband: "Not too much talking, now, he needs rest." She went out on to the landing, leaving the two men.

The chair was of the kind which could be almost horizontal or very upright, and Rollison gradually changed its position until he was sitting upright. Doing so, he caught a glimpse of his reflection in a mirror over the fireplace. He had three small patches of sticking plaster and several pinkish cuts which were little more than scratches. No one would doubt that he had been through the wars.

"Mr. R.," said Ebbutt, sitting on a wooden armchair, "that was nasty."

"But for you, it would have been nastier," Rollison said gratefully.

"I'm not going to dispute that," said Ebbutt. "What's on, Mr. R.?" when Rollison didn't answer immediately, he went on: "Who wants you dead?"

Rollison pursed his lips, and made a small cut by the side of his nose sting; but that did not prevent him from answering: "Do you know a man named Kimber?"

"Can't say I do. Who is he, when he's about?"

"I *think* he's the prime mover of an attempt to defraud the Income Tax authorities," Rollison answered.

"*Who?*" breathed Ebbutt.

"The Income Tax, or if you prefer it, the Inland Revenue people."

"Well, you can't blame anyone for that, Mr. R., can you? Bloody ruinous, these taxes are, never would surprise me if someone took the law into their own hands about it." When Rollison didn't respond Ebbutt went on: "Do you mean to say you're working for the taxman?"

Rollison snorted; and Ebbutt looked bewildered, his face between that of a handsome pig and a benevolent cow. His face was as remarkable as his figure. He had a small forehead and cranium but a broad face with jawbone to cheekbone. What chin he had was hidden by three rings or tyres of pale flesh. His shoulders sloped but he was enormous at the chest and even more massive at his middle; but he seemed to fade away to small thighs and delicate feet and ankles. He was clad in a white loose-knit sweater and a pair of baggy flannel trousers. His small lips puckered all the time, and his button of a nose twitched; and as he breathed he wheezed: it was a chronic affliction.

"Not exactly for the taxman," Rollison said. "In fact in the beginning ..."

Ebbutt was enthralled by the narrative. So was Lil, who brought in tea for all three and sipped and listened to the Toff. She often said she enjoyed just listening to his voice. There were noises from downstairs as the barmen cleared up after the night's business. Rollison short cut many of the corners but the story as it was told covered all significant details, and in many ways the recital refreshed his memory. He had started on his third cup of tea when the narration was finished.

Ebbutt said, explosively: "Blimey!"

"William, I would like you to moderate your language," Lil reproved, and she shifted forward in her chair, prim and upright. "Have you *any* idea what this Kimber is doing?" "

"Working on Inspectors of Income Tax, anyone can see that," scoffed Ebbutt.

"I mean *how?*" asked Lil.

"I don't know at all," Rollison said. "I only know that several have died in accidents, possibly because they wouldn't play ball, and others seem scared out of their wits. The obvious possibility is that they are being put under pressure to make them assess taxes on certain people or businesses too low."

"Well, like I told you, you can't blame no one—" began Ebbutt.

"Nonsense!" exclaimed Lil. "If they cheat Inspectors of Taxes they cheat the State, and if they cheat the State they defraud all the taxpayers. I do declare you get worse as you grow older, William." She pursed her lips and folded her hands in her lap, while Ebbutt, thoroughly used to this kind of reprimand and reproach, simply said: "Any idea how many firms, Mr. R.?"

"No idea at all."

"Now how much tax is involved?"

"Again – no idea," replied Rollison. "But Bill Grice has been working on this for some time and obviously thinks it's big. I am only guessing but it looks to me as if Kimber uses some attractive women" – he heard Lil say *"Hussies!"* in a whisper as he went on –

"and begins by seducing the Inspectors. It is anybody's guess, but man being frail—"

"Amen," breathed Lil.

"They probably get into debt or—"

"Bed," interjected Ebbutt.

"William!" barked Lil.

"Into trouble, anyhow," went on Rollison, "and certainly they can be blackmailed to fix certain assessments."

"You mean, if a man should pay a thousand pounds tax he only pays a hundred?" asked Lil.

"Or a hundred thousand and he only pays ten thousand."

"Do you mean there are men who earn so much money they have to pay a *hundred thousand pounds,"* breathed Lil.

"Daylight robbery," growled Ebbutt.

"Companies have been known to pay in millions," Rollison pointed out mildly. "One really big company whose tax was reduced by half because of the activities of Kimber and his friends could easily make the racket worthwhile. If there are a dozen companies—"

"It's just a huge fraud!" Lil said in an unbelieving voice. "It's a crime to have money like that when there are so many people starving."

"It's a crime to fix tax so high it makes this kind of racket worthwhile," Bill Ebbutt growled; and Rollison sensed that these two people, devoted to each other, often saw social situations from entirely different angles. "Anyway, Mr. R, one thing's plain as the nose on your face." He leaned back and waited to be pressed to explain what he meant; all the encouragement he received was Lil's sharp-voiced: "Well? What are you waiting for?"

Ebbutt snorted. "If you had any sense you'd be able to finish what I was going to say." He looked down his nose. "You've got them on the run, Mr. R. They wouldn't have laid on tonight's raid if you hadn't. They're scared stiff of you, trying to discredit you first and cut your throat afterwards. Amazing how that recording was laid on tonight. The devils appeared out of nowhere and disappeared into nowhere, too. There wasn't a single one left when the police arrived."

"And when was that?"

"Five minutes after they started to attack you," Ebbutt answered, and gave a wheezy little laugh. "I will say my old baskets did a good job, Mr. R. Coming out with those Indian clubs was a stroke of genius!"

"Bill," Rollison said quietly, "I owe my life to that stroke of genius."

"Forget it." Ebbutt waved his plump hands. When you come to think of what we in these parts owe you, Mr. R., it's nothing. Mind you if they'd known you were championing the taxman I don't know they would have been so quick off the mark!"

"William—" began Lil.

"Okay, okay, I was only joking," Ebbutt protested. "That's the trouble with you army folk, no sense of humour. Have they, Mr. R.?" He concealed a grin as he went on: "They'd put that tape-recorder on the bottle and switched it on just as things were getting interesting between you and Ding Dong. He's as tough as they come, Ding Dong is, but I didn't expect to see him here tonight."

"Why not?" asked Rollison, sharply.

"Well, blood's a hell of a lot thicker than water in that family," Ebbutt asserted. "And Ding Dong was really cut up about Daisy II. It's a funny thing how that family has stood together, the 'usband going away to quod for eight years or so breaks most families into little pieces. I suppose Ding Dong and Daisy just couldn't sit at home and watch one another, they had to come out. And the Blue Dog's as good a place as any, even if I do say it myself."

"Do you know where Violet is?" asked Rollison.

"She works nights, somewhere in the West End," answered Ebbutt. "I don't know more than that."

"How much do you know about Ding Dong?" asked Rollison.

"Well, there you have me," Ebbutt admitted. "I don't know a lot. He's the kind of cove you take for granted after a while. I don't mind telling you that when he was around here as a kid, I didn't have any time for him at all. Wasn't a bit surprised when he used a knife to cut up a man. But being inside taught him a lesson all right. Many's the time I've heard him talking to youngsters in the public bar, Mr.

R. 'Anyone who does a job that puts him inside is crazy,' he always said. 'Keep out of quod whatever you do.' And there's another thing, Mr. R. I've known him give a pony to some chaps down on their luck who were thinking of doing a job. 'Keep out of trouble,' he always advised them. 'But if you blow this and get broke again so that you have to do a job, don't come back to me for no more help.'"

Ebbutt stopped, frowning, as if he could not understand such a man as Ding Dong Bell behaving in such a way. Rollison turned all the new information over in his mind, and was about to ask another question when Lil said: "Prevention's better than cure, isn't it?"

"Who said it wasn't?" demanded Ebbutt. "Okay, Ding Dong has kept a lot of kids out of the cops' way. Do you know why I think he does it, Mr. R.?"

"No. Tell me," urged Rollison.

"I think he scores up a black every time he robs the cops of a case," Ebbutt declared earnestly. "All he ever thinks about is outwitting the police. Isn't that right, Lil?"

"For once I agree you *are* right," Lil conceded.

"How does he make his money?" asked Rollison.

"Dunno that he needs much," Ebbutt replied. "He's a carpenter and joiner, proper handyman, and he does a lot of the work in the houses around here. Kind of Handy Andy, if you know what I mean. Studies the gee-gees, and has a system which brings him in a bit of dough, too. And of course he gets a lot slipped to him when he hides someone."

"Hides?" asked Rollison.

"Whenever he gets the chance he hides people who are on the run from the rozzers," explained Ebbutt. "Everyone knows it but no one's really been able to prove it. He knows the docks like the back of his hands, and can finger places where men can lay low for a few days. He knows the masters of cargo boats who'll take a wanted man out of England for a price, too. Proper traffic in that, but you don't need telling, Mr. R."

"I don't need telling," agreed Rollison soberly. "How deeply is Ding Dong involved in this?"

"If you ask me, pretty deep," answered Ebbutt. "But I can't *prove* it, Mr. R. I can tell you another thing, though. The police are always on the lookout for anyone being kept under cover, and if they could fasten anything on to Ding Dong Bell they wouldn't lose a minute. But they can't. If they could they certainly would," added Ebbutt for extra emphasis. "I— "

He broke off, for the telephone bell rang. Like a giant sloth he heaved himself out of the armchair and crossed to the instrument in a corner. He looked so enormous from behind, at the seat almost twice as broad as at the shoulders and the knees. Lil moved and studied the cuts and scratches on Rollison's face, and then unexpectedly kissed him lightly on the forehead.

"You take care of yourself, Mr. Rollison," she pleaded earnestly. "There aren't so many men like you that we can afford to lose one."

Her eyes, sometimes smouldering grey, were moist; and she held his hands tightly, her fingers very cool. Above the things she said in her quiet voice, there sounded Ebbutt's as he demanded: "Who? ... Maybe he is, maybe he isn't ... Well, who wants 'im? ... *Who?* ... Oh, Mr. Grice, why didn't you say so right away? Just 'old on and I'll find out whether he's still here." Ebbutt turned, gave a gargantuan wink, and called in a loud voice as if to someone a long way off: "Anyone know if Mr. R. is still downstairs? ... Don't keep me waiting a lifetime, I've got Mr. Grice on the line ... Won't keep you long, Superintendent—"

Rollison got up and moved slowly towards the big ex-boxer and the telephone. Lil began to tidy up: towels, basin of browny coloured water, bottles of lotion, tin of adhesive plasters, antiseptic. She had these on a tray as Rollison reached her husband and took the telephone. At the same moment Ebbutt said hoarsely: "I've got him, Mr. Grice. Here he is." Rollison said: "Hallo, Bill."

"You mean you *are* alive," Grice said, sarcasm redolent in his voice.

"Don't say you're sorry to hear it," Rollison retorted mildly.

"No. Just astounded," Grice replied, and then he went on more seriously: "I'm told it was touch and go, and that you were badly cut about the head and face. Are you really all right, Rolly?"

"All my cuts and scratches are superficial," Rollison assured him. "I'm still capable of action, Bill. Is there anything I can do to help?"

"I don't know," Grice said in a quiet voice, "but I have had some reports, and they come from some documents left behind at Kimber's place in Jermyn Street; he hid some papers under floorboards, and didn't have time to take the boards up. Seven senior Inspectors of Taxes have been or are being blackmailed into being involved in some kind of racket. Two have died; one is in hospital after a car accident. The others, including the man Watson at Pleydell House, seem to be missing. Watson may turn up but he hasn't yet been home tonight. And each of these handles some particularly big private as well as company accounts. The Fraud Squad with some Inland Revenue investigators have started going through the major accounts at each office. Meanwhile, if you have the faintest idea where any of the missing officers are, I want to know."

After a long pause, Rollison asked quietly: "What makes you think I might know?"

"Because Kimber is trying so hard either to keep you quiet or to kill you," Grice answered. "He wouldn't do that if he weren't worried about what you know. What *do* you know?" Grice finished with an aggressive, accusing note in his voice.

Chapter 17

Question

There was a long pause, with the Ebbutts staring at Rollison obviously aware that Grice was being difficult, to say the least, and Grice breathing heavily as if he were waiting to pounce. At least he did not speak again, but allowed Rollison time to think. There was a ring at the flat door, which was at the head of the stairs leading up from the public bar. Lil waited for Bill to go, while he waited for her. Eventually he got up with great reluctance and Lil settled back in her chair.

"Bill," said Rollison quietly into the telephone.

"Yes?"

"I have no idea what I'm supposed to know."

"*I don't believe you.*"

"All the same it's true," Rollison insisted. "I haven't the faintest idea. Whether you believe it or not, I've always been a step behind in this affair, whereas Kimber, Grice and Company think I've been a step ahead. There is one thing I haven't told you."

"Ah!" cried Grice, in triumph. "I knew you were keeping something back! What is it?"

"Watson uses the name of A. W. Grey and has booked on the Harwich-Hook of Holland ferry tomorrow night," Rollison said.

"Are you positive?"

"Yes," Rollison said, and at least Grice had the grace not to ask him how he knew.

"Where is he now?" demanded Grice.

"I haven't the faintest idea."

"Or the other missing Inspectors?"

"I don't know a thing more," Rollison insisted, and as he pondered Grice seemed to bite on a retort, before saying: "Well, Kimber certainly thinks you do. Can't you rack your brains to discover what it is? In all the years I've known you I can't remember a time when you had information without realising what it was."

"I stand rebuked," Rollison said. "Bill—"

"Yes?"

"Do you know where Kimber and the girls are?"

"We've no idea at all," Grice assured him. "But what we do know is that Kimber was all set to disappear, and must have had a hiding place already prepared. Rolly, he's done his best to make you out a bare-faced liar as well as to kill you. You must surely know why."

"Obviously, I should," agreed Rollison forlornly, "but the fact is that I don't. Have you heard about the tape-recorder played at the Blue Dog?"

"Not only at the Blue Dog," Grice told him. "One was sent here to me by a special messenger whom we can't trace. At least three newspapers have received identical tapes, and the *Globe* appears to be eager to use theirs." A rough laugh sounded in Grice's voice, and there was a rougher note in his tone when he went on: "I'll be at the office until midnight at least. Call me if you have a flash of memory, won't you?"

"The very moment," Rollison promised.

He rang off as the other grunted "Goodbye", and replaced the receiver slowly and thoughtfully. Grice was not really convinced that he, Rollison, was not playing a double game, and when it came to the crunch this could mean lack of co-operation from the police. He must find a way to convince the Yard man. As that thought hardened, he heard Bill Ebbutt approaching, and a moment later Ebbutt, filling the narrow doorway, ushered in a girl the sight of whom gave Rollison such a shock that all thought of Grice and his doubts and suspicions were driven away.

For the girl looked like young Daisy Bell come to life.

There was no doubt at all: the likeness between this girl and Daisy was startling, and Rollison stood with his hand still on the telephone, heart thumping. As the girl came in, however, he saw that make-up skilfully covered the scars on her face. It gave to her attractiveness a slight artificiality; making her look rather like a doll. She caught the eye of Rollison on the instant and he could not make up his mind why she was so intent. She glanced once at Lil, and said in a husky voice: "'Evening, Mrs. Ebbutt," but she did not stop moving until she came within a foot of the Toff. The scent of her make-up was very strong, but even at close quarters the appearance was perfect. The eye-shadow made her eyes seem very bright, reminiscent of her father's.

Ebbutt stood and Lil sat behind her.

She said: "I hate you."

Rollison neither moved nor spoke.

"I hate your guts," she went on.

"A lot of people do," Rollison said quietly.

"I would like to cut your throat."

"As many others would," said Rollison. "What have I done to you, Violet?"

"Oh, not to *me,*" she breathed. "That's all you ever think about – what happens to *you.* You never think about other people, you're just the bloody egocentric Toff. And you think other people are all the same. But they're not. I don't care a flicking curse about what happens to *me,* but you've lied to my Dad, you've made a bloody fool out of him."

She broke off.

Tears were shimmering in her eyes. She spoke while hardly moving her lips, spitting the words out. Her hands were clenched by her sides; it was easy to believe that she would like to throw herself at him and beat and claw him about the face. She actually began to shake. Rollison saw Lil shift in her chair, saw her lips move as if she were about to interrupt, but Rollison raised his hand and she understood that he wanted to handle this by himself.

"What about your father?" Rollison asked, very quietly.

"As if you didn't know!"

"I don't know of anything that would upset you like this," he said, "unless Daisy's death—"

"You bloody liar! You know what you did."

"No, Vi," Rollison said in a very gentle voice, "I may be all kinds of things but I am not a liar. I don't know what's happened. I was delayed coming to see him—"

"*Delayed!* You stayed away, that's what you did, to help the cops."

"I was kept back," Rollison said. "Not by or for the police but by a man named Kimber." He couldn't tell this girl in her present mood, that for a while he had actually forgotten the appointment with her father.

"All you do is lie," she said flatly.

"What happened, Vi?" Rollison asked, still gently. "If I know I might be able to help."

"Help him back inside, you mean!"

Rollison pursed his lips, and moved past the girl to the Ebbutts's. There was a great deal of uncertainty in his mind but he was sure that Violet Bell was genuinely distressed. Yet – she was wasting time, almost as if deliberately. Could she be fooling him? Could she want to keep him here for some reason he could not even begin to guess? He heard her turn round but did not look at her as he said: "I haven't time to waste, Bill. If she tells you what's happened, call me at my flat, will you?"

"Glad to, Mr. R." Ebbutt looked worried, nevertheless.

"That's all you can bloody do, run *away!*" screamed Violet. She sprang at Rollison who turned in time to push out an arm to save himself. But she struck out with the other hand and caught one of the scratches with her fingernail; it hurt, sharp, tearing. She flung herself bodily at him, striking wildly, until he managed to get both arms round her and held her tight. She writhed and tried to kick, but without much vigour, and suddenly she went limp in his arms, and began to cry.

He remembered her father's tears.

He stood quietly holding her, not trying to quieten her sobs, not patting her or soothing her. Lil Ebbutt went out of the room, Bill stood by the door, his expression much less troubled. The tension easing from the girl somehow eased it from them all. Soon, Rollison moved towards Ebbutt's big armchair, and lowered Violet Bell into it. He took a handkerchief from his pocket and placed it in her hands. Soon, she was dabbing her eyes and sniffing; then in a kind of defiance, gave an enormous blow, honking loudly. Suddenly she laughed in spite of herself at the unexpected sound, and Ebbutt also laughed. Rollison drew up a leather pouffe, brought back by the Ebbutts after a tour of the Middle East, and looked up at the girl.

"I know," he said. "I am hateful and egocentric. Most of the time I wish I wasn't."

"You're—you're a beast!" she cried from behind the handkerchief.

"Yes, of course. But what have I done this time?"

"You *must* know!"

"I've no idea," he assured her. "You gave me half a clue just now but not enough for me to build a case on."

She dabbed her eyes again and drew the handkerchief away. The eye shadow had smeared, so had her lipstick, and there were several smeared patches in the matt make-up. At one spot beneath her left cheek part of a scar had been uncovered. She looked at him searchingly, and said: "The police searched our house while Dad was here at the Blue Dog."

"*Searched* it? What for?"

"They've always persecuted him and they always will."

"Only if he deserves to be persecuted."

"That's a bloody lie and you know it!"

"All right, Vi," Rollison said. "There are bad policemen as well as good ones. Let's not argue about whether your father sometimes asks for trouble, just tell me what happened tonight."

"You promised to come and see him at half-past nine."

"I know. I'm sorry—"

"Oh, you half-wit!" Violet cried. "Don't you know what you did to him today? Don't you know he came to your apartment ready to kill you, he blamed you and the cops for killing Daisy. God knows how but you did something to him. You made him like you – you, a friend of the police, a copper's nark, he *liked* you. And you made him begin to think that there were some decent coppers. That Grice, for one. I've never seen him like it before, and – and Mum's been trying to make him see like this for *years*. Lately I have, too."

Rollison thought: Good Lord!

Lil Ebbutt appeared with a tea tray but she made hardly a sound as she placed it on a table and sat down in an easy chair. Violet was staring with great intensity at the Toff, and he was suddenly and vividly aware of what she was telling him.

She was nearly sobbing as she went on: "All he could do was *hate*, don't you understand? Oh, not Mum and me and Daisy, there isn't a kinder man alive – why, look what he did for *me*. He offered to send me to university, told me to study as long as I wanted to, nothing was too much trouble and nothing cost too much. But the police—" she drew in a deep breath, paused, and declaimed as if she were at a public meeting: "How—he—hates—the—police. He *hates* them – do you understand?"

"Yes," Rollison said, gently.

"He blamed them for everything that ever went wrong in our family. For his troubles – and for these!" Without warning she scrubbed the left side of her face with the handkerchief until the make-up came off and the scars showed, livid.

"Violet, they couldn't—" began Lil Ebbutt.

"Oh, yes, it was their fault, you don't know anything about it! I was scared of a man who threatened to cut me up, and I went to the police and asked for protection. The next bloody night this happened, but they didn't pin it on him. Protection! All they ever protected is their own backsides so they can sit down while they eat!"

It must have been two or three years ago.

It was likely that the police hadn't taken the threat seriously, or that some officer detailed to watch her had been careless. Whatever the explanation it was easy to see how the wounding must have affected this girl, and how it had happened, how it had hardened the hatred which her father already had for the police.

"Now can you really understand how much he hates the cops?" Violet choked. 'And—and it was eating into him. He'd been bad enough before but he was ten times as bad after this happened to me. It didn't matter what Mum and me said to try to make it easier, he—he had only to see a police uniform to start going pale. And he had this neuro-dermatitis, do you know what that is?"

"A rash and itching due to nervous strain," answered Rollison.

"That's about it," Violet agreed. "Goes all red in big patches when he sees coppers sometimes, and if ever he got a chance to help a man get away from the police, he took it. It didn't matter what Mum and me said, he took it."

"What about young Daisy?" asked Rollison.

Violet frowned, and brushed dark hair back from her forehead.

"Daisy was different," she answered. "Daisy didn't worry about anything but having a good time. That's the truth. Dad was always worried in case she got into trouble." Violet paused and then gave a shrill hoot of laughter. "Not *that* kind of trouble, Daisy and me always knew our way about! Trouble with the police, I mean. He has a kind of obsession, neurosis, call it what you like. He always thinks that if one of us girls got in trouble with the police they'd make it as hard as they could for us just to get back at him."

Ebbutt, quiet for so long, blurted out: "Crap, that is – cr"You can call it what you like but that's what Dad thinks," asserted Violet with great conviction. She looked more impressive now, with the make-up smeared and the scars revealed, than she had when she first came in. "And it didn't matter what Mum or I said, it made no difference. He was eaten up with hate, he was getting worse all the time. When—when Daisy was killed, he nearly went mad."

Violet's voice dropped to a whisper, and for the first time since she had recovered from her crying spasm she looked away from Rollison, and dabbed at her eyes. She soon recovered again, however, and went on: "Mum was home with him when we heard. She was cut up bad enough but she had to think about *him*, can't you see? She telephoned for me at a friend's place, and I was home within the hour. He was still on the rampage, we thought we'd have to get a doctor to him. Then someone else telephoned him and told him you were involved. He quietened down, then. I thought he'd decided to kill you, Mr. Rollison."

"Did you?" asked Rollison quietly.

"Yes, I bloody did! We wouldn't have let him out if we'd known for sure he was after you, but he seemed a lot better, and we went into the kitchen to make some tea. He slipped out."

She dabbed at her eyes again and was silent for a long time. Lil took the opportunity to pour out tea, and brought the tray to Rollison and the girl. Violet took a cup, splashed in milk, and went on with her story while holding the cup and saucer on her lap.

"When he came back, it was like a miracle. It really was. I don't know what you'd said to him. He'd been picked up by the cops and this Grice talked to him as if he was human. I tell you he was a different man, and he couldn't wait to see you tonight. Made me stay in so that I could meet you, too. And – you didn't turn up. You didn't phone or do anything, you just let him down. He waited nearly an hour and came over here, and as soon as his back was turned the cops got into the house. They were still there when Dad got back. I—I'd been to see my boyfriend," she went on, "I didn't see any point in staying home, and I don't like pubs. Mum came round for me, and told me what had happened, and I came straight to see you, Mr. Bloody Rollison Bloody Toff. I hope you feel proud of yourself."

After a long pause, she began to sip her tea; the cup and saucer trembled in her hand. Rollison sipped the strong, hot tea, watching her. He waited until she seemed to have control of herself again, and then asked: "Where is your father now?"

"At home."

"Are the police still with him?"

"Yes. Three of the so-and-sos."

"Have they found anything at the house?"

"How the hell could they – there's nothing there."

"Not even a guest or two hiding from the police?"

"My God!" Violet exclaimed. "How did you earn your reputation? You don't think he'd hide anyone in his own home, do you?"

"Then where would he hide them?"

She paused again and put her cup down sharply, leaned back in the chair and stared at him with her eyes narrowed to slits. Ebbutt, wheezing, downed his tea and whispered to Lil.

"I gotta go and lock up."

"Don't be long, dear," Lil said, glued to her chair.

"Not a sec longer than I can help!"

Ebbutt went out of the room faster than he had moved for a long time, making surprisingly little sound for so big a man. Lil moved to the girl and took away her empty cup, and Violet had not said a word when she returned with the refill. But as she took it, she said in a low-pitched voice: "So you're clever. You think I'd tell you where he hides them, don't you? Well, I won't. I won't do a thing to help you in your dirty coppers' business, Toff. But if you've any decency in you, you'll go and get the coppers off his neck. If you do he might listen to you, but if you don't—" She drew in a hissing breath and then raised her voice and shouted: "If you don't help him, *I'll* cut your throat if it's the last thing I do!"

Very slowly, Rollison got to his feet, saying: "I'll go and see him right away, Violet. I don't know what I can do to help him, but at least I'll try."

Chapter 18

23 Quaker Street

A police car stood outside Number 25 Quaker Street.

A dozen or so people had gathered at a respectable distance; no one spoke. Now and again a distorted voice sounded over the walkie-talkie in the police car; now and again a car passed, people walked, or an aeroplane flew overhead so that the flashing green and red navigational lights were visible.

Rollison and Bill Ebbutt turned the corner.

Ebbutt had come to take Bell's wife away, so that Bell and the Toff could talk together. A uniformed policeman moved from the doorway of the little house as they drew up, recognised Rollison, and drew back.

"Good evening, sir."

"Good evening. Is Mr. Bell in?"

"Yes, sir – but no one except the family is allowed in unless Mr. Grice or Mr. Hunter has given permission. Mr. Hunter's in charge at Division, sir."

"Thank you," Rollison said. "May I talk to Mr. Grice over the walkie-talkie?"

"I certainly don't see why not," the policeman agreed, and moved towards the car. The crowd, also recognising Rollison, drew nearer. He wondered whether stones or broken glass would come hurtling, but nothing did. The policeman got *Information* and *Information* found Grice, who sounded preoccupied as he said: "What is it?"

"I would like to talk to Ding Dong Bell on his own," Rollison said. "As far as I can gather he's being held under a form of house arrest."

"Who—" began Grice, only to break off. "Oh, it's you. Hold on a minute." Grice's voice sounded as he talked to someone on another telephone but Rollison caught only a word here and there and had no idea whether the other conversation was about this case. Then Grice returned, very brisk and forthright. "One or two facts you should know, before you do anything. We picked up Watson, your Inspector of Taxes. He wasn't going to the Hook of Holland – that was to fool anyone who followed him, he was at London Airport. But the name 'Grey' on his passport helped us."

Rollison grunted: "Good. Has he talked?"

"Fairly freely. He has been under pressure to accept false returns from a number of private individuals and companies. At first, he refused: then he was tricked into a compromising situation with a young woman, and threatened with blackmail. The two pressures together broke his resistance."

"I can imagine," Rollison said. "Found the other Inspectors?"

"Not yet, but there will be a much fuller report later," Grice said. "Meanwhile, Watson says that he had to contact a man named Bell. Ding Dong Bell." Grice paused long enough for that to sink in and went on gruffly: "At the Blue Dog."

Rollison drew in a sharp breath.

"That seems as good a place as any."

"Apparently Ebbutt's place has been used for a rendezvous frequently – or so Watson was told." When Rollison didn't reply, Grice went on: "And obviously there are a lot of people in Bell's pay who live near the Blue Dog – live or have hideouts. They nearly got you tonight, didn't they?"

"Yes," Rollison conceded, "but—"

"There aren't any buts about it," Grice interrupted, either impatient or angry. "Obviously Bell set them on to you. Obviously Bell is providing hiding places for criminals who want to get out of the country. It's the most convenient place in London, you can pick up a ship for any part of the world there, and Bell has been in the district all his life. I did wonder for a few minutes this morning whether we'd misjudged him, but we haven't. You will make the biggest mistake of your life if you put any faith in him, Rolly."

Rollison said quietly: "You could be right."

"Over this, I *am* right. Do you still want to talk to him alone?"

"Yes," Rollison said.

"Don't let him lie his way out of any situation," Grice warned. "And—just a moment, my other telephone's ringing."

Again Rollison heard him speaking without being able to catch the words. He leaned against the side of the car, watching the crowd, which had grown much larger. He wondered again if any among the crowd would start hurling stones or bottles; perhaps the presence of the policemen discouraged them. He let everything Grice told him soak into his mind, and tried to picture Bell's face, that morning, and Violet's face as well as her impassioned words. Somewhere buried here was a truth he did not yet even begin to understand.

But he could understand Grice, whose voice was suddenly loud in his ear.

"You there?"

'Yes, Bill," answered Rollison meekly. "What were you going to give me dire warning about next?"

"Rolly," Grice said, "we can't trace Kimber and the women who were with him. We had some addresses, but all the places are empty. They must be in hiding somewhere. As the London docks make one of the best escape routes they may be somewhere near the docks. Bell is an expert in such hideouts, and it is virtually certain he is involved in this affair. He *must* know where Kimber and Company are. What's more, they may have records of the tax frauds they've perpetrated – at least a full list of the Inspectors on whom they've used pressure. Many millions of pounds could be involved. We *must* get our hands on Kimber."

"I couldn't agree more," Rollison agreed.

"As far as we can judge, Bell is the one man who can tell us where he's hiding," Grice went on. "He won't talk to us. He might talk to you. If you're allowed to talk to him it will be on condition that you tell us - tell me - everything you find out. Is that clearly understood?"

Grice, several miles away in the heart of London, seemed to be in this very street. Ebbutt stood still but the wheezing of his breath was the loudest sound in Rollison's ears. He really had no choice, of course, and wasn't sure that he would want to do anything different, and yet in a way it seemed almost a form of betrayal of a man who appeared to think of himself as one who could trust nobody.

"Are you there?" asked Grice, and he went on before Rollison could reply: "You can't have any reservations about this, Rolly."

"No," Rollison admitted. "No. Some doubts as to procedure but none about the principle." He gave a snort of a laugh. "All right, Bill. Oh—may Bell's wife leave to go to the Blue Dog?"

"Yes. There's no restriction on her movements."

"Good," said Rollison, and added emphatically: "Very good. All right, I'll do what I can."

He actually began to replace the receiver before Grice spoke again and yet the new tone in the Yard man's voice sounded very clearly, and Rollison put the receiver to his ear again, to hear Grice in midstream. He knew that Grice meant exactly what he was saying; sensed and believed the anxiety in his voice. The silence in the poorly lit street seemed intense; it was as if William Grice and he, Richard Rollison, were the only two men in the world.

"Don't have any doubt at all," Grice was saying. "This man is extremely dangerous. Hatred has built up in him for years, and he probably sees you as even worse than a policeman – as a citizen who needn't work with us yet often chooses to. He could kill you, Rolly. If you are there with him absolutely alone there's nothing I or anybody else can do to help. You realise that, don't you?"

"Fully," Rollison said.

"And you realise that you don't have to go?"

"I go of my own free will," Rollison said quietly. "And I know what the odds are, Bill. Thanks."

He replaced the receiver.

There was a strange stillness and a strange stirring in the street. Then Ebbutt went to the door and knocked, and Detective Sergeant Moriarty opened the door, saying: "I heard all that on my transistor. I'll send Mrs. Bell out, but I want to be here when Mr. Rollison and Bell meet."

Rollison nodded agreement.

Soon, the older Daisy Bell was coming along the little passage, a short woman who seemed to have a good figure and who certainly had nice legs and ankles. She passed the Toff, obviously not recognising him, then suddenly spun round; the likeness between her and her two daughters was quite remarkable.

She exclaimed: "It's Mr. Rollison!"

"That's right," Rollison said.

She stood as close to him as Violet had, and – so short a time ago – as Daisy II; and the light of a nearby lamp fell on to her face. She actually stretched out her hands and took his, while the police officers hovered very close as if they expected her to attack the Toff.

"Help him," she pleaded. "Please help him."

Then she turned and, head held high, walked to Bill Ebbutt. Before Rollison entered Number 25 Quaker Street, the sharp sounds of her footsteps and the heavy ones of the ex-prize fighter sounded very clearly. Rollison followed the policeman. A second man whom he had seen before Detective Officer Odlum, stood in the doorway of a small room, where Bell stood in a far corner. Odlum stood aside to allow Rollison to pass. Bell stared at him, eyes glassy bright, and did not glance away when Moriarty spoke from the passage. He was close to Rollison, who felt something cold and metallic against his hand. Suddenly, he realised it was a small walkie-talkie transistor radio. He slid it into his trousers pocket, locating the switch before he let it go.

"No tricks, Bell. Understand."

Bell didn't answer Moriarty.

"If you kill Mr. Rollison," Moriarty went on with unexpected depth of feeling, "you'll be sent down for the rest of your life. Don't you forget."

For the first time, Bell stirred; for the first time his lips moved. And for the first time he spoke.

"Some things would be worth it," he said in a grating voice. "Wouldn't they, Toff?"

And the way he uttered the name turned it into a sneer.

Moriarty stood looking back over his shoulder, with the other man just behind him, close to the open front door. Watching Bell but acutely aware of the policeman's presence, Rollison said: "I've even known things worth dying for."

"Mr. Rollison," Moriarty pleaded, "don't take any chances. And remember we'll be just outside."

"Thank you." Rollison sensed the tall man's real concern, and his reluctance to leave the little house. But the front door closed at last and silence followed while the two men in the room contemplated each other. "Would you like to go and make sure that the door's locked?" Rollison went on. "They're capable of leaving it on the latch so as to get back in a hurry."

"So you don't trust them, either." Bell didn't move. "I'll take a chance. If anyone steps on the doormat now, I'll know." He moved to the tiny, red brick fireplace and put down a switch. "Even poor men sometimes need a burglar alarm system."

Rollison nodded.

Bell demanded: "What brought you, nark?"

"Two things," Rollison said. "Your daughter's request, and Grice's."

"That's a bloody lie! Vi wouldn't—"

"Violet came to Ebbutt's place and made it obvious that you thought I'd stayed away so as to give the police time to search this house. I convinced her that I hadn't and she asked me to come and try to convince you." Rollison paused but when Bell showed no reaction he went on: "Grice thinks you've hidden Kimber and his girls. He knows you won't talk to him or any policeman but he thinks you might talk to me."

"So that you can pass it on to the police?"

"Yes."

"Not bloody likely!" Bell rasped, but there was a half- smile on his face. "My God, I almost believe you're honest!"

"You can be sure I mean what I say," Rollison said.

"So what kept you tonight?"

"Kimber putting on the performance you heard at the Blue Dog."

"Now don't come it – that wasn't tonight, it was days ago!"

"I don't know what Kimber told you," Rollison said, "but that little scene was put on tonight. The idea was to make me look a fool."

"It succeeded," jeered Bell.

"Kimber cut out those passages which made him look the bigger idiot," Rollison said mildly. "It was done well and it was done quickly. Bell—" His voice sharpened.

"Yes?"

"Did you put the recorder on the 4X bottle?"

"No."

"Did you arrange the attack on me?"

"No."

"Who did?"

"Kimber. He told me I'd hear the truth about you sooner or later. He sent a message while I was at the Blue Dog."

"Why did he try to kill me as well?" asked Rollison. "I can understand him wanting to make a fool of me. I can understand him wanting to kill me. And I could understand why you would want one or the other. But why both?" He kept silent for several seconds and then his voice positively boomed: "Do *you* know?"

Bell moistened his lips.

"Yes."

"Why?"

The other man turned round, not slowly but with a controlled movement, and opened a wall cupboard fixed a little below his head level. Inside were bottles and glasses. He took out Scotch whisky, a soda syphon and two stubby glasses which seemed to be of cut glass, and set these on a table by his side. Without a word he began to pour out, and when both glasses held a generous tot of whisky, he asked: "Soda?"

"An inch from the top, please."

Bell squirted in the soda carefully, showing no signs of unsteadiness. He filled his own glass with about the same amount and carried Rollison's across to him. He stepped away and raised his glass.

"To the cop-haters," he said, and drank.

"To all good policemen," Rollison said, and sipped.

"So you persuaded Violet that you didn't fix it so that the police would come here and search?"

"If you used your head, you'd know I didn't."

"Meaning?" Bell's voice hardened.

"If I wanted you out of the house I would have arranged to meet you somewhere else. And in any case the police would have searched whether you were at home or not. Do you know the truth about yourself?" Rollison asked in a mood between casual and earnest. "You're so full of prejudice there are times you don't even let yourself think. When a man wears dark glasses, everything is dark; and you can wear dark glasses over your mind."

"*Very* clever," sneered Bell. "Next thing you'll tell me you didn't arrange the attack on yourself so as to make it look as if I fixed it."

"I didn't arrange it," Rollison answered, briskly. "Grice thinks you did. I think Kimber alone or Kimber with you did. You were going to tell me why I was both to be ridiculed and killed. Remember?"

"So I was," agreed Bell in a smooth voice. "And so I was. It was so you will get it both ways. If you escape alive then you'll be made a laughing stock. If you're killed it won't matter a damn whether you look a fool. The idea is to make sure you're not taken seriously. To make sure no one will ever take you seriously again. I told Kimber I wanted to make you look a fool first. I didn't say anything about killing you, only about threatening to kill and so frightening the life out of you." Bell drained his glass and turned to the bottle, adding: "Don't tell me you're not frightened out of your wits."

Chapter 19

Onslaught

Rollison sipped his whisky and soda, eased himself down into an armchair, crossed his ankles and smiled. No man in his senses could even imagine that he was frightened. He took out cigarettes and placed the case on the side of the chair; but made no attempt to select a cigarette.

"Guess again," he said.

"All right; you're not scared." There was a note of admiration in Bell's voice. "That doesn't mean you shouldn't be." He poured himself another drink, and went on: "So Grice wants you to make me talk and tell him what I say."

"Yes," agreed Rollison. "But he doesn't have to know what I'm going to say to you."

"Well, say it." Bell's voice came over the glass which he raised to his lips; it had exceptional lucidity.

"I want you to tell me where Kimber and his harem are hiding, and I want you to give yourself up and make a statement to the police saying that for years you've been hiding men and finding ships on which they could sail out of the country," Rollison said flatly.

Bell opened his lips and almost gasped: "Now I know you're mad!"

"I mean it," Rollison insisted.

"They'd put me in jail for the rest of my life!"

"I don't think they would."

"You know damned well they would!"

"No I don't," retorted Rollison, sharply. "I think you could turn Queen's Evidence and get off with a nominal sentence even if the police brought proceedings."

"Queen's Evidence – *me!*"

"You. Ding Dong Bell."

"To save my skin?" Bell almost screamed.

"To save a few years of happy life for you and your wife and your surviving daughter," Rollison corrected and went on with a note of savagery: "If you're caught and put away, what's life going to be like for Daisy? It will be bad enough for Violet, but for Daisy it will be purgatory. And it won't help her if you're rotting away in a cell eating your heart out with hate for the police and the warders, the judge and the jury. If your wife has a chance it will have to be because you give it to her. And it will carry a chance for yourself at the same time. I don't see what else you can do, do you?"

"I can tell you and the cops to go to hell!"

"And your wife and Violet?"

"You leave them out of this!"

"They can't be left out," Rollison retorted. "You can't ignore your family because it happens to suit you. You couldn't even on an issue of principle, but this isn't principle. It's a question of whom you really owe loyalty to: Adrian Kimber or your wife and daughter."

Bell was fingering his glass as if trying to hide the intenseness with which he was listening. His deep-set eyes burned as Rollison had seen before and they were undoubtedly a reflection of the hate which burned within him. Rollison could imagine what a tremendous effort he was making to keep his self-control; how heat and fury were rising up in him like a volcano about to erupt.

Quietly, deliberately, Rollison went on: "You know it was Kimber who killed your daughter, don't you?"

Bell ground out: "That's a lie! *You* drove her to her death!"

"Bell," Rollison went on, "how much longer are you going to fool yourself? Or let Kimber make a fool of you? Kimber—"

"Shut your trap," Bell grated.

"Bell—"

"Or I'll shut it for you!"

"Bell," Rollison went on in a quieter voice than before, "sooner or later you've got to face up to the fact that you can't go on living by shouting other people down. And you can't go on living by shutting your ears to what other people say: your wife, for instance, or Violet. You've got to start listening."

"I listened to you this morning and where has it got me?" growled Bell.

"To a chance to rid yourself of lifelong hatred. A chance to live without a chip on your shoulder. A chance to be a man instead of a ghost of a man."

Bell moved with sudden and devastating speed, hurled his glass against the wall and as it shattered hurled himself at Rollison as his daughter had done not long ago. But this man was like steel. Rollison smashed a blow at him but Bell got beneath his guard, kneed him savagely in the groin, and then clawed at his neck. His fingers bit in like steel claws. His thumbs pressed against Rollison's windpipe. He leaned forward with all his weight so that Rollison was half on and half off the arm of the chair. The shimmering eyes were close to Rollison's, who had never been in a fiercer grip nor been in greater danger.

But he was fully conscious and alert.

He knew that if he fought back Bell would go berserk and would not stop until his fingers had squeezed the life out of the man whom he saw as his arch-enemy. Yet the temptation to kick, strike out, struggle, was overwhelming. Keeping still was like giving up without a fight: and giving up life. Somehow he held his breath, and held himself rigid, arms and legs limp, body as limp as it could be while he was held this way.

He could not breathe.

The blood thundered through his head and pumped like a dynamo through his ears.

His lungs seemed full to bursting. Bell's face was distorted because of his own distorted vision. The eyes were like pools of venom and the turned-back lips were like a wild creature's. Rollison thought in despair that he had judged the man wrongly, that he should have fought back from the beginning.

He couldn't breathe.

His lungs felt like bursting.

The thumbs at his windpipe were like burning bands of steel.

He felt his eyes rolling and felt consciousness slipping away; and he realised that he had no one but himself to blame. He was far beyond the point of no return. Grice had warned him, so had Moriarty. Jolly's plea "Be careful, sir, I beg you to be careful" echoed in his ears. So did Kimber's voice and the laughter of the girls at Jermyn Street.

And then, the pressure stopped.

He felt as if red hot air was tearing down his windpipe and into his lungs, but it *was* air. He felt a swelling pain at his throat but not the awful pressure. He felt his body being moved until he knew he was slumped back into the easy chair, head against the back, whole body, arms and legs limp. A combination of pain and pins and needles and numbness spread all over him. He could only gulp down air, and each time his lungs seemed to burn and swell. It was an age before he began to breathe more normally, and to open his eyes to the room and to Bell. Bell now stood by the wall cupboard, glass in hand. By his side was a glass of 4X. He brought this across to Rollison as Rollison sat more upright, and more at ease.

His hand was trembling as he took the beer, but the glass was filled to the brim, and none spilled over.

He sipped; the beer was at room temperature, thick, soothing. He coughed, choked, sipped again, and at last uttered a word.

"Thanks."

"I don't know why I didn't choke the life out of you," Bell said.

Rollison took another, longer drink, and schooled himself to say: "You're a better man than you think you are."

Bell snorted. "And still a sense of humour!"

"Anyone—anyone who's been as near death as that and pulled out of it ought to have plenty to laugh about," Rollison replied. "May I walk about?"

"Suit yourself," Bell conceded.

He stood watching as Rollison put the glass on a small chair, placed his hands on the arms of the one he was sitting in, and gradually rose to his feet. His head had seemed to swell and at the same time to feel like a drum; empty, yet filled with booming sounds. On his feet he swayed, stretched himself with a great effort against the chair arm, and staggered so much that it seemed as if he would have to give up. But at last he took a step forward; another and another. He made two turns round the room, and stopped at the door.

"I'd like to wash."

"I'll show you," Bell said.

The bathroom was tiny but modern and well-equipped. Rollison could see how the two houses had been converted; the room next to this was the kitchen. At one time in such a place the privy would have been outside and a cold tap would have been the only water supply. He ran hot and cold and looked at himself in a large mirror in front of which were women's toiletries and a few oddments obviously belonging to Bell.

His face was a mass of small scratches, plaster patches, and red spots mixed with pale ones. A thorough mess. He rinsed it carefully, dabbed himself dry and went back to the other room. Now, Bell was sitting down, as relaxed as Rollison could remember seeing him. He looked through narrowed eyes at Rollison, who felt stiff at the neck and swollen at the larynx and yet much more himself.

"So I'm a ghost of a man," Bell said.

"You're a very solid ghost," Rollison said ruefully. "How old are you?"

Bell was startled into saying: "Fifty-one."

"Twenty good years are waiting, if you'll let them."

"This Queen's Evidence, you mean?"

"Yes."

"That would turn me into a squealer. What kind of life could I live that way?"

"Bell," Rollison said hoarsely. He took another gulp of 4X and had to make an effort to go on: "It's your one chance; I meant what I told you. If Kimber and his party get away then you'll be charged with helping them escape and you'll get a long sentence. There won't be any kind of life left for you or your family. You needn't shop another soul, either – just Kimber's group. No one is going to have any sympathy with them when the whole truth is known. And remember—"

Rollison broke off.

Bell looked calmer but there was no way of being sure how he would react to what Rollison had to say; *had* to say, for it seemed the one thing which might sway him into doing what Rollison wanted. Rollison moved back to the chair and sat on the arm, positioning himself so that if Bell did become aggressive again he would be in a better position to fight back. And this time he would fight with all the strength left in him.

He said: "Kimber was responsible for Daisy's death. You can't help him to escape if you want an easy conscience: you'd never be able to live in peace if you let him go. You don't really have any choice, and you must know it." He saw Bell tensing himself in the chair as if ready to leap to the attack again, but went on: "Turn him in, Ding Dong."

He himself was ready to leap.

Bell rose slowly to his feet, and his breath hissed through his nostrils and about the room.

"Toff," he said.

"Yes?"

"I'll tell you another thing I can't do: turn Kimber in *and* stick around. If I turn him in I've got to get out of the country myself. I'm not going to turn Queen's Evidence, only a fool would expect me to."

Rollison's heart began to thump with a swift burst of hope. This was the first time Bell had shown any signs of cracking, and once a tiny crack came he might split wide open in a burst of emotional revulsion. His lips seemed very dry and obviously he had great difficulty in getting the words out.

Rollison said: "One thing's certain; you will have to live with yourself."

"Toff," Bell said again, as if a great fight were being waged within him.

"Yes?"

"If I turn Kimber in and then get out of the country, will you look after my wife and Violet?"

So he *was* on the verge of giving way! Properly handled, now, the situation could turn from disaster to triumph; not for him, Rollison, but for law and order and justice. Rollison's heart had seldom beaten so fast.

He said: "Do you mean—money?"

"No, you flicking fool. I've made sure they'll have enough money. I mean, will you stop the police from hounding them?"

"With absolute certainty," Rollison promised. "Yes. Not that I think they'll try."

"One other thing," Bell rasped.

"Yes?"

"Will you help get them out of the country if they want to join me?"

"Yes," Rollison answered very quietly. "Everything I've got, everything my friends have, will be used to help them. I mean that absolutely."

He stood up.

Bell looked at him hard and long as they stood facing each other. There seemed no sound in the room, no sound at all outside. Then slowly, Bell put his right hand forward, arm extended but bent upwards a little. Rollison put his arm forward. He knew he had won: in this strangest of all his cases, he had worked on the mind and heart of a man, not on his body and his fears, to get what he knew was vital. There was still a possibility that Bell would turn on him at the last moment, that the bent arm was really tensed to grip, twist, fool the Toff.

"Shake on it," Bell said.

Rollison gripped his hard, cold hand. There was no hint of a trick, only the grip of a man who was sealing his promise with a handshake; a man accepting this handshake as a full and binding agreement: Bell to say where Kimber was, Rollison to 'look after' Daisy Bell and Violet.

"My word on it," Rollison said, quietly.

"It's a deal," Bell replied as they gripped hands. Something like an electric shock ran through him, for Bell was quivering as if every nerve he had was tense and taut, almost raw with the effort he had made to reach this decision.

As they stood there, as they released each other, the pact between them made, as Rollison wondered whether he would ever know such a moment again, as he wondered, also, whether he or Bell would make the next move, there was a click of sound; then a buzzing; and as Bell looked upwards, astounded, a voice – *Kimber's voice* – came from the ceiling. The ceiling was opening over the wall common with the house next door, and the voice came even louder.

"The only deal you've got is with me, Bell. Don't move! Don't either of you move! Or I'll blow this place and everything in it to kingdom come. And if you don't believe me—"

Something small and bright like a glass phial, fell from the gap in the ceiling, and struck the arm of the chair Bell had been sitting in. It burst with a sharp explosion. There was a vivid blue flash, out of the flame a great balloon of blue smoke. Dazzled, and half-blinded, Rollison turned and groped for the door, but the smoke caught at his mouth and nose and made tears stream from his eyes.

"Now listen to me, Ding Dong Bell," Kimber went on savagely. "You get me and my party away or your precious wife and her Violet won't live the night out. And nor will you. The bloody Toff won't, either, you didn't reprieve him for long."

All this time the gap in the ceiling widened, and Kimber and two other men dropped down into the smoke-filled room.

Chapter 20

The Microphones

The sounds now were of the men dropping, moving about, steadying themselves. One was by the doorway, to make sure neither the Toff nor Bell could escape. Kimber himself, with that raw blond Viking look, was standing and grinning, anger softened by his moment of triumph. The smoke thinned, and Rollison could see clearly. One man close to him, a pistol in his hand; others close to Bell, also holding guns. And Kimber was equidistant from both Rollison and Ding Dong Bell.

Bell was looking at Kimber; there was no way of judging what he was thinking.

Rollison slid his hand to his trousers pocket and switched on the walkie-talkie. There were no atmospherics, and Moriarty would surely have the sense to make sure the set wasn't used from the street.

"You're both fools," Kimber said in a gloating voice. "You're a bigger fool than Rollison, Bell. Did you really think I'd trust you? When you brought me and my little family to the Meeting House along the street and let us into two houses next door by the roof, did you think I'd just wait for you to come and let me out?" He gave a guffaw of laughter. "I did some investigating. Toff, did *you* know that all the houses from here to the Meeting House are connected above the ceiling? That you can get into each one by the ceiling or the door? That's a fact. And when Ding Dong Bell is planning to hide runaways for a day or two or a week or two he takes them to the Meeting House where they're supposed to work for the printer or a radio and television repair shop, and then they disappear. Right, Bell?"

"When their ship's ready to sail, they're taken on board," Bell said thickly.

"Like I would have been," Kimber cried.

"I had three ships ready for your party," Bell said. "For the morning tide."

"They'd better still be ready!"

Bell said: "No, Kimber. The deal's off."

"You took the thousand pounds—"

"You can have it back," Bell said. "It will help to pay for your defence."

Kimber said savagely: "We'll sail, or your wife and daughter—"

"You don't think I'd believe you'd let any of us live now, do you?" Bell asked. "When you killed Daisy—"

"I didn't kill her!"

"Oh yes you did," Bell said coldly. "The moment you involved her in your tax frauds, you killed her. Until you started on her she was clean, absolutely clean. You lured her into your 'family' as you call it, and from then on she didn't have a chance."

Kimber was breathing through his nostrils, harshly. Rollison was alert for every move, every change of expression, every word of explanation. He stood so still that even the man watching him looked beyond him to Bell and Kimber, who stood like two duellists, lunging with words, cutting new wounds and opening old ones.

"So she didn't have a chance?" Kimber breathed. "She would have, but for Rollison." He glanced at Rollison but only for a moment. "She would have, but for Rollison, I tell you!" His voice rose. "If he hadn't run after her from the tax office—"

"You'd got her where you wanted her, before then," Bell growled. "She was one of your harem, in it for kicks, high on drugs like all the others – and driven to do what you wanted because she had to have the shots and you made her earn them. My Daisy wouldn't have gone spying and sneaking if she hadn't been desperate."

"Your Daisy was a sexy little bitch." Kimber lashed with his tongue, as if all he wanted to do was hurt. "All the same, if the Toff hadn't followed her she wouldn't have had to run. I sent her to listen so as to make sure whether Watson said anything to the Toff. I called him and warned him not to but I had to be sure. He didn't. All that worried the Toff was his own tax. If he hadn't chased after Daisy—"

"Why was the driver of the M.G. killed?" Rollison asked, out of the blue. And Kimber answered almost on a reflex, so simply that it did not occur to the Toff that it was anything but true.

"He was an accountant who worked for me, but he fell in love with Daisy. He was waiting there to pick her up and started after her when she ran into the road. I was there with my wife, but I wore a beard. I spoke to my wife and the driver recognised my voice. He was so scared he drove straight on and killed her. And then my wife gave him a shot of curare through a blowpipe which looked like a cigarette."

"You mean that if Daisy hadn't been killed by the car she would have had a poisoned dart, too," said Rollison, coldly.

"She was getting too scared and she and her boyfriend were too dangerous," Kimber almost boasted. He seemed to think it did not matter what he said, he was so sure of his ascendancy over the others.

"And was Johnny P. Rains getting dangerous?" Rollison demanded.

"He poked his nose in too far," Kimber replied roughly.

"Just as you did, Toff. If you'd kept your nose out we could have gone on with this for a long time." He turned to Bell and rasped: "We still can, if you play ball. No one else need know about these hideouts. Just get us away and there'll be no more trouble. When things have quietened down I can come back and start again. I'll tell you what," went on Kimber, "I'll give you a ten per cent cut in all the profits. It's fool proof, Bell! I find someone who will give me a cut in what they save on tax. Then I get a tax inspector where I want him and *he* reduces the assessment, or accepts a false statement of accounts. I tell you it's easy."

Bell said: "I can see that."

"And all we're taking the cash from is the Exchequer – most people would do that any day of the week. Why, they can afford fewer cops, Ding Dong! Look at it that way!"

Kimber laughed.

Whether he meant what he said; whether he would have worked with Bell again, there was no way of telling. And that was not Rollison's chief concern. Whatever those men decided, he would be condemned; and they had no idea that all that was being said was also being heard outside.

Even if the police raided there would be grave danger from him, and he could not escape that danger. At this moment he did not want to. The great issue was in Bell's mind. What would he do under this kind of pressure? There was no way of telling from his expression. It seemed as if both guns were turned on him now; as if everyone here felt that the Toff did not matter: only Bell could decide the issue.

He did not look away from Kimber.

"You don't need any more telling," Kimber urged. "My way you can always get back at the cops. The other way the cops come out on top, and that won't be any easier to take just because the Toff's dead and buried."

"No," Bell admitted. "It won't."

"Ding Dong," Rollison said quietly, "if you go along with Kimber, your wife and Violet won't have a minute's peace, Kimber will always have you under his thumb. He'll get dozens of decent girls and have them hopped up and get them working on tax inspectors or anyone he wants to rob and cheat."

Kimber roared: "Shut your trap!" And he roared: "Put a bullet in his guts—"

The men with the guns jerked to attention, both of them swivelled their weapons towards Rollison. He did the only possible thing and dived for the man nearest him, but even if he were put off his shot the other wouldn't be.

He heard a shot.

He wasn't hit.

He heard a cry, and saw the man in front of him swing the gun away. Then Bell appeared, like a bullet, braving the gun now turned on him. In those few wild moments Rollison realised that Bell had disarmed the first man and was grappling with the second; that

Kimber was clawing at Bell's neck, trying desperately to drag him off. The first gunman was in a heap on the floor, his gun two feet away from him. Rollison bent down and picked up the gun. He struck Kimber across the head with the butt, and as Kimber fell and Bell pinned the other gunman helplessly against the wall, there was thunderous banging on the street door, and a crash before the police came rushing in. In seconds, Kimber and the gunmen were handcuffed, and Moriarty was climbing up into the roof. Other police, alerted by the walkie-talkie messages, had already surrounded the old Meeting House, and Kimber's wife and the girls were arrested there.

In the narrow passage, Rollison was close behind Bell, and he whispered in his ear.

"I can create a disturbance, and you can get away. It's your last chance."

Bell said in a tired but steady voice: "I'll see it out now, Toff. I'll find out for sure if the cops will give me a square deal."

"If they don't," Rollison said very clearly, "I shall never work with them again."

It was noon next day, after Rollison had breakfasted late and taken his time in telling Jolly what had happened, when the telephone bell rang. It had been ringing most of the morning, mostly calls from newspapers but also one from Bill Ebbutt and another from Violet Bell. There had been a pause and Rollison hoped this call would be from Grice; he was very anxious indeed to hear from Grice.

It was Ding Dong Bell.

"Okay, Toff," Bell said. "I'm going to turn Queen's Evidence. I've made a statement. Your friend Grice isn't going to bring up any of the other cases where I've helped people out of the country." There was a laugh in Bell's voice. "He says if I help anyone else out illegally he'll throw the book at me, but Q.E. this time wipes the slate clean. You satisfied?"

"Are *you* satisfied?" Rollison demanded, but he already knew the answer.

"All I can say, Toff, is that you've done a good job of cleaning up the cops. They're a big improvement on what they used to be. Now I'm going to phone Daisy. I wanted you to be the first to know about the deal."

"Ding Dong," the Toff said warmly, "I couldn't be more glad."

Bell rang off without another word.

In the weeks that followed the Fraud Squad finished its enquiries and showed that the amount of income tax money which would have found its way into Kimber's pocket was fifty per cent of some three million pounds. Eleven tax offices were affected, and over twenty officials, each a victim first of blackmail and then of threats of violence. The trial, when it came, would probably last for weeks.

Before the trial, on a day when he was to go and have a meal at the Bell's after a call at the Blue Dog, Rollison went to see a newly promoted official, once Watson's deputy, the man named Cobb. There he was with his droll smile but completely free from aggressiveness or any hint of accusation.

"Between these four walls, Mr. Rollison," he said, "you *were* wrongly assessed, and by me. I put a new interpretation of those expense figures. No trouble at all to clear it up, and your assessment will be just about halved."

Rollison, greatly relieved, stared at him thoughtfully, before saying: "That was an odd kind of mistake, wasn't it?"

"Very easy one to make," said Cobb, beaming. "And it had one good effect, Mr. Rollison, didn't it? It made sure you became involved in the mystery! I knew Mr. Watson was in some kind of trouble, and I didn't want to tell the police or my superiors. So— "

"You mean you fixed those figures so that I would find out Watson was a worried man?" gasped Rollison.

"Shhhh!" breathed Cobb, with his most expansive smile yet. "Everyone's liable to make a little slip now and again. I'm only too glad to be able to put it right, Mr. Rollison. In fact, I've got your revised assessment here."

JOHN CREASEY

GIDEON'S DAY

Gideon's day is a busy one. He balances family commitments with solving a series of seemingly unrelated crimes from which a plot nonetheless evolves and a mystery is solved.

One of the most senior officers within Scotland Yard, George Gideon's crime solving abilities are in the finest traditions of London's world famous police headquarters. His analytical brain and sense of fairness is respected by colleagues and villains alike.

'The finest of all Scotland Yard series' – New York Times.

GIDEON'S FIRE

Commander George Gideon of Scotland Yard has to deal successively with news of a mass murderer, a depraved maniac, and the deaths of a family in an arson attack on an old building south of the river. This leaves little time for the crisis developing at home ....

'Gideon of Scotland Yard emerges as one of the most real working detectives in modern fiction.... A sympathetic and believable professional policeman.' - New York Times

JOHN CREASEY

THE CREEPERS

"The prisoner's hand was thin and bony ... And in the centre of the palm was a pinkish mark. It was the shape of a wolf's head, mouth open, fangs showing. Although it was what he had expected to see, Inspector West felt a twinge of repugnance a stab not unrelated to fear. It was the fifth time he had seen the mark of the wolf – the mark of Lobo."

A gang of cat burglars led by Lobo cause mayhem as they terrorize the city. They must be stopped, but with little in the way of evidence the police are baffled. Just how can Inspector West manage to do this in what is a race against time before more victims succumb?

"Here is an excellent novel of law enforcement officers, harried, discouraged and desperately fatigued, moving inexorably ahead under the pressure of knowledge that they must succeed to save human lives." - Cleveland Plain-Dealer

"Furiously exciting" - Chicago Tribune

"The action is fast, continuous and exciting" - San Francisco News

JOHN CREASEY

INTRODUCING THE TOFF

Whilst returning home from a cricket match at his father's country home, the Honourable Richard Rollison - alias The Toff - comes across an accident which proves to be a mystery. As he delves deeper into the matter with his usual perseverance and thoroughness , murder and suspense form the backdrop to a fast moving and exciting adventure.

'The Toff has been promoted to a place of honour among amateur detectives.' – The Times Literary Supplement

CASE AGAINST PAUL RAEBURN

Chief Inspector Roger West has been watching and waiting for over two years – he is determined to catch Paul Raeburn out. The millionaire racketeer may have made a mistake, following the killing of a small time crook.

Can the ace detective triumph over the evil Raeburn in what are very difficult circumstances? This cannot be assumed as not eveything, it would seem, is as simple as it first appears .....

'Creasey can drive a narrative along like nobody's business ... ingenious plot ... interesting background .' - The Sunday Times

Printed in Great Britain
by Amazon.co.uk, Ltd.,
Marston Gate.